# SONGS OF KHAOS

## GODS OF HUNGER COMPANION TALES

R.M. VIRTUES

Cover by Covers in Color

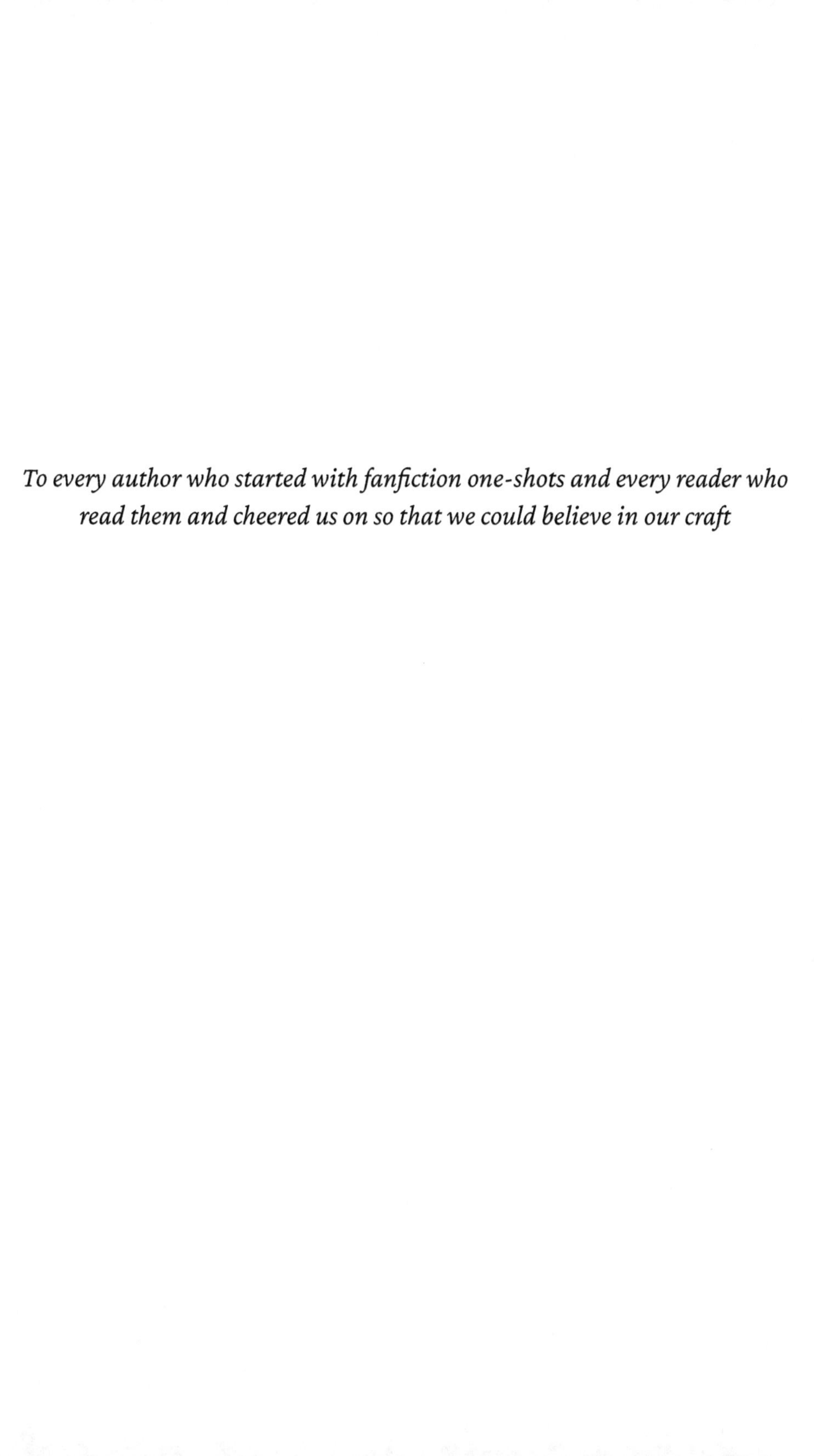

*To every author who started with fanfiction one-shots and every reader who read them and cheered us on so that we could believe in our craft*

# I

# SEDUCTIVE IN SILK

## HADES & PERSEPHONE

The ceiling in Hades' penthouse was not quite as high as Persephone's old apartment, much less as high as that of the Pantheon Theatre. Nonetheless, she had found a way to practice her routines among the silks Apollo had professionally installed in one of its few spare rooms not yet claimed by one of Hades' nephews and nieces. Through his skilled efforts, the architect had managed to create a wonderland within the confines of these four walls, each of which now housed full-length mirrors that covered every inch of them. In this way, Persephone was able to critique herself, to adjust her movements and placements until everything was perfect. A routine did not leave this room until it was perfect.

She spent most of her mornings in this studio once Hades departed for the casino downstairs. Though now that he was leader of the entire city, he left the casino altogether more often. It wasn't excessive, perhaps a couple times a week, but it was more than he was used to, which meant it was more than she was used to. Regardless, waking up next to him was a sure thing, and he made sure to spend quality time with her —and on her— before he left. Not that this always kept them from seeking the other out for a quick fix throughout the day.

She laid her weight over two vibrant red silks, each looped beneath her thighs and shoulders. She had been off the ground for nearly an hour now after taking the time to stretch and properly hydrate. Entering this space was much like entering another world, and being on the swings brought her to center.

In the months while the Pantheon was being repaired, her makeshift stages had hardly held her over, her anxiety only just tempered by Hades and their family. Now that shows had resumed at the Pantheon and ground had broken on a new performance center, the sky was the limit, and Persephone found herself falling in love with the process all over again.

Before she could begin the elegant flip of her body, the door opened behind her. Like clockwork.

Tilting her head, she found a perfect view of Hades entering the room in one of the mirrors. His tie was already hanging free over his shoulders, the top few buttons of his dress shirt undone and his suit jacket lost somewhere earlier in his walk through the apartment. There was a look of stark determination on his face, a look that sent shivers down her spine and through to her toes. Seph smirked, stretching out like a cat across her silk hammock.

He'd only been downstairs a few hours, but she supposed she should be proud. He usually didn't even last that long. Neither of them did. They were always looking for an excuse to corner the other. Several months together had done nothing to temper that need.

"Did you forget something?" Persephone asked, bowing her back until she could look at him upside down.

"I do believe so, but perhaps you can confirm."

"I will do my best."

"Did I by chance tell you how absolutely stunning you are before I left this morning?"

"Hm." A look of contemplation crossed her features. "You know, I can't say for certain that you did. That's alarming, isn't it?"

"Very."

She sat up, snaking her arms through the silk and twirling slowly to face him. He was much closer by the time she did so. He placed his hands just above either of hers, curling them around the silk and pulling her closer. Persephone wrapped her legs around him, locking her ankles behind his knees. Their mouths hovered a mere inch from one another, breaths mingling in the minuscule space between them. His eyes darted down to her lips. Her eyes stayed on his.

"You keep this up, and people might start to talk," she whispered.

"Mhm, and what do you suspect they'll say?"

"That the new leader of Khaos Falls has a weakness."

"I don't need to keep this up for them to figure that out."

"They'll say you're easily distracted then, constantly abandoning your post to do naughty things with an employee."

"You're technically not my employee. We simply share a work-space. Calliope is your boss."

"And what do you think my boss would say if—"

To her utter delight, he didn't let her finish, pressing his mouth firmly against hers. She sighed, all but melting into him, pulling him closer with her legs. His hands slid down to lay over hers briefly before he retracted completely, working to remove his shirt. Using him to keep herself upright, she reached for his belt, undoing the buckle with expert efficiency and unbuttoning his trousers in the same swift motion. They fell down around his ankles, and she shoved his boxers along after them.

She reached back up, winding her hands in the silks once more and waiting patiently. Fates, he looked devastating, his breathing already heavy and his eyes burning with want. His palms ascended her thighs once he'd removed his shirt, pushing her skirt out of the way until he could hook his fingers into the hem of her panties. He met her gaze, the message clear. Gripping the silks tighter, she lifted herself up into the air high enough so that he could peel her panties from her legs.

"Didn't wanna rip that pair too?" she jabbed playfully.

"No, I did, but... Your upper body strength is very arousing to me."

"Is that right? So..."

Lowering herself again, she rolled her hips against his, earning a grunt. Her lips curled, the swollen head of his stiff cock pressing into her thigh. She moved closer to him, her lips brushing his jaw.

"Are you saying you wanna watch me - ride you like this? Lifting myself up and lowering myself down on your dick?"

He swallowed. Hard. "Well - yeah, now that you mention it, that would be lovely."

She dragged her tongue over his skin, replenishing the taste she failed to manage too long without. A guttural sound vibrated against her mouth, traveling up his throat and manifesting into a growl.

"Put your hands on mine," she instructed softly. "Don't let go."

As soon as he did what he was told, she made her move. With a slow roll and rotation of her hips, she managed to slide onto his shaft, clamping down around him intermittently throughout her gradual descent.

There was a sigh of relief although she could not tell which one of them had provided it, her heels digging into the backs of his calves. She nipped at his neck, just below his thick beard, savoring each hiss and groan he afforded her. Tightening her hold on the silks, she ascended once more, raising her hips until she was poised at the tip of his dick.

"That's my girl," he mumbled before taking his turn to ravish her neck.

She purred at the scrape of his teeth along her skin, finding her rhythm with a mindless ease. Wind all the way up and slide all the way down, each stroke costing them the last dregs of their collective patience. Of course, that was the point. She would do anything to get him to that point, where he lost all desire to maintain his composure. And with each touch, he let her monitor his progress. He bit down, sucking hard at her pulse point until her back was arching, her clothed breasts pressed against his bare chest.

"Hades - fuck!"

That may have been what set him off, what pushed him off the edge and into desperation. Or maybe it was the glimpse of them he caught in the mirror when he raised his head. Either way, his hands fell from hers, taking her thighs in a possessive grip and slamming their hips together.

She gasped. He grunted. Their gazes, hooded and hazy, collided with the calamity of warring blades, sparks igniting from within them. He still looked at her like some brilliant phenomenon he was seeing for the first time. Even in his insatiable hunger, the awe was there, profound amidst any superficial lust he may have harbored. But no. It was always all for her. Hades spared her nothing, and she adored him for it.

He claimed her lips again, his tongue sliding across hers as he reared back and rammed into her again. Her shrill cries were muffled by his mouth, but he pulled back the moment she went to reach for him.

"Uh uh." He shook his head. "Don't let go of those."

She had a mind to argue, to point out that he had disobeyed a similar order, to test his resolve and see what he might do if she disobeyed too. He seemed to pick up on that instinct however because he immediately retracted his cock. It was obvious he was going to slip out completely, but before he could, she grasped the silks and drove him back into her with her heels.

Something between a hiss and a chuckle left him, and while he was momentarily stunned, she began to ride him again, lifting herself up and winding herself down before grinding her hips hard into his. He pressed his palms along the swell of her ass but did not manipulate her movements, allowing her to maintain control. Trusting he would continue to do so, she let her head fall back, giving herself to the gentle swing of her body and the gruff satisfaction Hades mouthed against her throat.

The familiar high she derived from being in the air was now fused with the unearthly ecstasy Hades always brought her, and it was a dimension of euphoria she had never known. She leaned back, swinging her hips into his and building her momentum in the process. All the soreness he'd left her with earlier that morning was long gone, leaving only need in its wake. Need that he fulfilled with a vengeance.

"Fuck, Seph—"

She knew he was close, and not just to the edge. He was close to losing his composure. And this, that moment just before it slipped through his fingers like ice turned to water, was her favorite part.

She slowed just enough, not too much that he reprimanded her but enough that his hips began jerking forward in that sloppy and unsynchronized way. He was chasing her mouth, the look in his eyes absent his commonplace pragmatism. It was wild and untamed, the flames behind his irises now raging infernos that set her alight. She could hardly keep her own eyes open and out of the back of her skull. It was a battle she quickly lost when he ducked his head and started nipping at her breasts through the fabric of her tank top.

"Hades! Fates, don't stop. Do not!"

He didn't seem to need the warning however. His hands now slid beneath her thighs, spreading them open further before they trailed up along her calves to her ankles. Slowly, very slowly, he continued to push her legs further apart until she was doing a split in the air, the stretch adding to the heat pooling in her belly. He held her like that, fucking her with a newfound eagerness that had each stroke accompanied by a grunt that continually grew in volume.

She could hardly hold on, her knuckles sheet-white around the silks.

He was nothing short of desperate now, the clap of their skin connecting echoing loudly through the space. She tiptoed on the edge of oblivion, her mind a mess of heat and color. And the one time she managed to open her eyes, they fell upon the delicious image of Hades' ass in the mirror, clenching with each thrust, the hard muscles in his thighs and calves evident and impeccable. His broad shoulders did the same, the definition there an art piece. One that could ruin her. She screwed her eyes shut.

She must have been slipping because soon, Hades had his hands under her, holding her as he continued to thrust.

"Let it go, babygirl." His voice was like a hot fire poker pressed into her skin. "Cum for me."

A cry of frustration tore through her teeth, so eager to please him as well as herself. That voice alone, smoother than the silk in her hands and by now just as familiar, made her toes curl and her breath catch. She ground down into his short and quick strokes, and he bent forward further so that each stroke offered substantial stimulation to her clit. It didn't matter where they were or how they did it, he was consistently in tune with her body and all its needs. And he fulfilled them before she could even think to ask.

"Now."

His possessive snarl was a tipping point —or rather a hard shove — into climax. Her body locked up, shaking and shivering, the heat consuming her without mercy. Her orgasm coiled around her neck and chest like a large serpent, stealing her breath, a bright white light exploding behind her eyes. It clutched her in its grasp for seconds, minutes, hours until at last, she came apart. Though mere moments later, she began to unravel again.

Hades was still drilling into her, his face contorted in determined focus and his nails digging into the small of her back. Frantic and feral, he plunged deeper into her cunt with a symphony of wanton sounds spilling from his lips. She released the silks —or they released her—

and wrapped her arms around his neck, holding on as he took what he needed and offered it back tenfold.

He had certainly become more comfortable with her in that he was no longer afraid to lose himself and relinquish control. She loved when he dropped the reins and did all the things he wanted to do to her exactly how he wanted to do them. No more holding back, no more taking it easy. She had all of him, and she would never again settle for anything less.

"Hades! Please!"

He stood up straight, palming her ass and guiding her way again. She fed on his desperation, fueled by his frantic movements in search of the perfect position, the proper angle. Her fingers hooked into his short hair, her breathing labored from both the remnants of her orgasm, the buildup of another, and the elusive nature of his. Moans turned into shouts turned into screams, Hades' roars underlining them all.

She came again from the sight of him, his eyes narrowed and eyebrows drawn down and teeth bared as if in warning. She shuddered against him, her pussy spasming as it gathered him in a vice grip, and then he was cumming too, his thrusts short and sharp until his hips stuttered to a stop.

She collapsed against him, letting her head fall upon his shoulder where his hand met it quickly. He cradled her in his arms there, kissing her temple. And there it was, that unbridled affection he always offered her after fucking her senseless. He was always affectionate of course, but after rough sex, he touched her like an apology, one he had no business making but one she cherished nonetheless.

"You think you can get through the rest of the work day now?" she hummed after what felt like ages, her eyes closed.

"Mm, I think I can make it through lunch."

She giggled, hugging him tighter. "Good... But if you can't, you know where to find me."

"You're damn right I do."

# 2

## A PROMISE

### HEPHAESTUS & DEIMOS

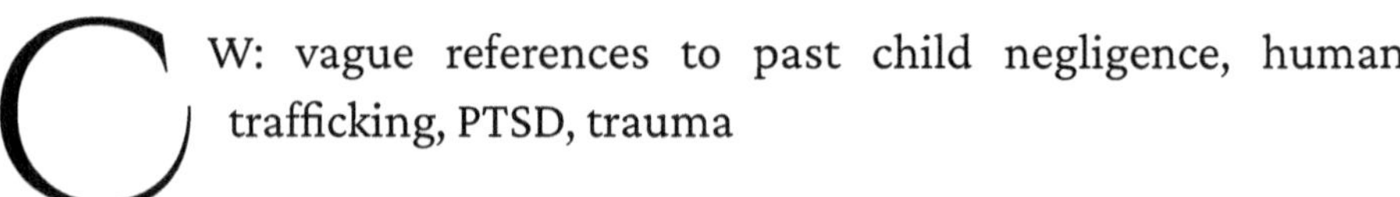

CW: vague references to past child negligence, human trafficking, PTSD, trauma

"Deimos?"

Hephaestus rubbed the sleep from his eyes as he entered the den, peering over the back of the couch to see Deimos sitting there with his knees drawn up to his chest and his chin resting atop them. He was illuminated by the light of the TV, but he looked smaller than usual, curling in on himself as much as he could. It was as though he was trying to disappear.

"What are you doing awake?"

Deimos shrugged, but as Hephaestus rounded the couch, he could see that the boy's face was glistening with freshly swept tears. Immediately, Heph assumed that Deimos had had a nightmare. While they had grown less frequent in the past month, especially now that they were living in Aphrodite's house rather than the upper floors of Lush,

Deimos still had them every now and again, and Hippocrates had informed Heph and Aphrodite that it would take some time before he stopped having them altogether. Stability would be key, second only to patience, and Hephaestus was doing his best to ensure both.

"Did you have a nightmare?" Hephaestus asked cautiously, sitting beside him.

Deimos shrugged again, his eyes still fixed on the TV screen. It wasn't at all uncanny for him to shut down like this, but Heph had believed they were both getting better at talking. Although he was fourteen, Deimos hardly looked it, with his thin baby face and soft curls and this innate ability to minimize the space he occupied. Where his twin brother seemed to have bounced back quite quickly from the things they had endured, it was painfully evident that Deimos had left so much behind in his past life as a prisoner. Hephaestus wanted to ask, but Hippocrates had warned against it, and Heph hadn't been keen to question the good doctor. Besides, he wasn't sure he could handle those answers just yet, not when there was nothing he could do to change them.

"Persephone will be here bright and early, you know," Heph went on, trying to sound conversational. "She's excited to take you to the museum. Aphrodite will be with you, so don't worry. Then you get to meet their mom. Well, Persephone's mom, but she raised Aphrodite too, so... Oh, and her Aunt Hestia. You'll probably like her more than you like Demeter, and honestly she'll probably like you more too, but that's more because of me not you. But be nice all the same, alright? Unless she's not nice. Then she's asking for it."

Hephaestus smiled, but Deimos only nodded, still refusing to look at him. Yet that wasn't what drew Hephaestus's acute attention. Deimos had visibly begun to shake. Panic rose like bile in Hephaestus's throat.

He could admit he had no idea what he was doing. He was reminded of it each and every day, and it would be unfair to the twins to say otherwise. It had less to do with upbringing and more to do with the rigid, longstanding belief that he would never be in this position. It was all trial and error for both him and Aphrodite, raising these two boys, but he knew one thing for sure. He would rather figure it out than give up.

Still, he wished he knew. He wished he was as resolute in his parenting as he was in his security detail. Above all, he wished he could be certain that everything he was doing was the best thing for them. He didn't want to be another name on the long list of people who had failed these boys.

"But - if you get tired of being out at any moment, you don't hesitate to call me, okay? I'll drop everything I'm doing, and I'll come get you. Though I'm sure if you just tell Aphrodite you wanna come home, she'll listen. Whatever you need, okay? Just—"

"Will you warn us?"

It took Hephaestus more than a moment to realize Deimos had spoken, his mouth hardly moving, and even then, he wasn't sure he understood the question posed.

"Will I warn you about - what, Deimos?"

"When - when you send us away again. You won't... When our dad left us, he promised to be right back, but he lied. I just want to be told the truth this time."

Hephaestus's brows knitted together. "But - I thought you never knew your parents. Phobos, he said that—"

Deimos shook his head. "We promised each other we wouldn't talk about them, but - but... they both left us. Our mom, she left us with our dad because he had no money, and she wanted a lot of stuff. So then - our dad, he sent us to the pier, said we had to find work."

"But those men found you. Picked you up."

Deimos swallowed hard. "They told us that - they paid him to let them have us, that he wasn't coming back. And I knew it was true because he packed our backpacks before... Phobos didn't wanna believe it, so I let him pretend, but I don't pretend. I can't. Because I see them when I go to sleep. Not just the men, my parents too. So - just tell us. If we have to leave, I - don't want to see you when I sleep."

Hephaestus was silent for a long while, chewing the inside of his cheek. This was one of those answers he hadn't been ready to face. He wasn't entirely sure what to say in response, but he knew what he wasn't going to say. He wasn't going to say yes. He wasn't going to agree.

*They need a home. They need* us.

Aphrodite had been so sure when she'd said that to him, like two teenage boys was the easiest responsibility to take on after they had only been dating a couple weeks. He knew it was that big heart of hers, unwilling to let her pass up an opportunity to help. After all, she'd taken Eros in when she was nearly a kid herself, so how could this possibly be anymore difficult in her eyes?

Besides, the twins were far better behaved than Eros.

Nonetheless, Hephaestus hadn't been as certain as her at the time. While he did want to help them, he hadn't been convinced that they were the right people to do so. Or at least, that he was the right person.

But if Aphrodite was committed to it, and she wanted to do it with him, he wasn't going to turn away a blessing he once thought out of reach. He loved her, and he cared deeply for these boys. If he could do for them what Hades and Charon had done for him and his brothers, he would do it. By any means necessary.

"Deimos, we're not sending you away."

Deimos finally looked at him, a sharp glare in his eyes as if daring Hephaestus to lie to his face. Heph didn't back down. He reached out for Deimos but stopped short, instead turning his hand over and offering it to him. Deimos simply stared at it.

"Aphrodite and I, we - we want you to stay here with us," Hephaestus went on. "For good."

Deimos inspected his face with scrutinizing eyes. "—Why would you? We're broken."

Hephaestus was already shaking his head, tears stinging the corners of his eyes. "No. You are not broken, Deimos. I know you've seen broken things. You know what they are. Broken things don't fight. Broken things don't get up and walk away."

"But we—"

"You have pieces missing. We all do. Fates know I do, and I cannot promise you I will be perfect at this. I cannot promise you that I will never make a mistake or upset you or let you down, but I can promise you that I will do everything in my power to give you a good life from here on out. And that if I do mess up, I'll listen when you tell me how."

Deimos seemed to chew on that for a long while before he spoke again. "You protect people. That's what you do, so even if you've never been a dad before, I think you'll be a good one. But - we've never been anyone's sons. What if we're not good at it?"

Hephaestus bit down on his tongue, choking down the anguish threatening to overwhelm him. He had to be able to face this reality where he couldn't prevent what had happened to them in the hands of Acrisius. He had to accept that he only had control of what happened now.

"Well, I do know that a lot more goes into being a father than protection. And maybe you've never been anyone's sons because the ones who were offered that blessing weren't worthy of it, but I'll tell you this. You've been really great at it these past few weeks, and I would not trade either of you for anything."

Slowly, Deimos grinned until he was doing so with his entire face. He at last put his hand in Hephaestus's, and Hephaestus grinned too.

"So why don't we give it a try?" he suggested. "Because listen, Aphrodite has grown really, *really* attached to you both, and it would break her heart if you didn't stay with us."

"Okay, don't go half lyin' to that boy!"

Both Deimos and Heph jumped, turning to find Aphrodite standing in the mouth of the hallway beside a grinning Phobos.

"Tell him the *whole* truth," Aphrodite urged, leveling Hephaestus.

Heph smirked, looking back at Deimos. "And I've grown pretty attached to you too, so I'd like it if you and your brother would stick around."

Deimos nodded, his cheeks streaked with fresh tears. "Yeah, I wanna stay."

"And you know I do!" Phobos shouted. "Eros promised he would teach me how to—"

Heph threw up his hand. "Okay, but no lessons from Eros until Aphrodite and I have reviewed his curriculum."

The twins looked at one another, wide-eyed before Phobos spoke in a stage whisper.

"He even sounds like a dad."

Aphrodite smirked. "Oh, he's just warming up."

"Hey, we're a team, Aphrodite," Heph warned. "Don't go conspiring with the kids."

She shrugged. "I like to keep my loyalties loose."

She hugged Phobos to her side just as Deimos launched himself forward, throwing his arms around Hephaestus. Although caught off guard, Hephaestus managed to get his arms around the boy, a smile spreading across his scarred lips. While he had always expected to get more than he'd bargained for since agreeing to be Aphrodite's bodyguard, he had never expected this. Nor was there anything in the world he would trade it for.

"You promise you won't leave? Or send us away?" Deimos whispered.

Hephaestus hugged him tighter. "I promise. No matter what, Deimos, there is nothing you can do to make us stop caring for you. For as long as you live, this is your home."

# 3

# SAY SOMETHING

## HEPHAESTUS & APHRODITE

CW: trauma, PTSD

*Repetition breeds routine.*

That had always been one of Demeter's favorite "affirmations", mainly because that was as close as she ever came to an affirmation. And Aphrodite had never been like Persephone, who quickly became able to sort the good from the bad and the bad from the useless. When Seph left for school the first time, she only packed the things she needed from the notes her mother passed along. Back then, Aphrodite was only upset one of those things wasn't her. Now, she was mad that she hadn't taken notes of her own.

Instead, Aphrodite internalized everything and could only ever hope that when it came time to utilize one of Demeter's criticisms or reject it, the choice didn't upend her life.

*Repetition breeds routine.*

Coincidentally, this was also one of the more harmless mantras Demeter had bestowed upon her, and at the moment, it was becoming rather useful. Because each night, when she awoke screaming in a bed that was now far too big for one person and far too small for all of her worry, she knew what to do.

*Step one: Slap hand over mouth.*

This kept her from waking the twins down the hall. Of course, that was reliant on the hope that their own demons hadn't already torn them from sleep. They were still growing accustomed to their new home on Aphrodite's estate among so many other changes, so sleep was not yet a sure thing for any of them.

*Step two: Find phone.*

She usually fell asleep with it in her hand, thus leaving it at the mercy of her sheets and edges of the bed once she dozed off. However, once she found it, she could stare at the candid photo she'd taken of Hephaestus and the boys on their first trip to the beach two weeks ago until her heartbeat slowed to a standard rate.

If that took too long, she could scroll through the rest of the photos from that day, tending to land on the one of Hephaestus grinning ear to ear in a way she thought him incapable of while Phobos spiked his hair with seawater and Deimos strategically built a sandcastle beside his legs.

*Step three: Text Hephaestus and ask him when he's coming home in a way that that doesn't sound needy but still has some note of desperation because you are still learning that you need not manipulate emotions — yours or his— to get what you need from him.*

He was still overseeing the night shifts as they rebuilt Aphrodite's security team, meaning he was rarely home but for a few hours during the day. Part of her—the parts that had clawed out of the ruins of her father's home—feared this was his version of running away from her and his commitment to the sudden family he'd been given but hadn't planned for. The other part of her—the parts of her that had fallen in love with him and their new life—knew better.

That didn't make the nights any easier though because he didn't always text back right away. Actually, he didn't always text back, period. Sometimes, he would just show up fifteen minutes later with a hot mug of tea and some stupid joke she would laugh at because she loved him and not because it was actually funny.

But he always showed up.

And then she would pretend she didn't need him to baby her even as she burrowed into his side and mumbled 'thank you' into his armpit. And sometimes, that led to other things like her eager hand down his boxers and his possessive mouth on her neck.

...Okay, it *usually* led to that if the kids weren't awake too, but that was how she dealt with her emotions. Sue her.

*Repetition breeds routine. And routine, my darling daughters, is the key to a fruitful life.*

The second part of Demeter's mantra was not as helpful as the first in this situation, but it followed out of habit nonetheless. Of course, the entirety of it was the last thing on her mind when she first awoke, forcing her way into the waking world from the kind of nightmare that made it difficult to differentiate between the past and the present, the dream and the waking. The bodies and the blood and the bark of Acrisius's laughter in her ear... The darkness of her bedroom did nothing to assure her it wasn't real.

*Step one!*

She clapped a hand over her mouth, tears cascading over her palm and rolling down her wrist. Her lungs fought to expand and inflate, her nightgown plastered to her skin with cold sweat, the room around her far too still and yet spinning so fast that she couldn't find her bearings.

*Step two!*

She lunged towards her bedside table, searching for her phone, and when she was certain it wasn't there, she fumbled for the lamp. Then the door opened behind her slowly, and she bit down on her tongue, attempting to stifle the sobs clawing up her throat. She continued searching for her phone, no longer wanting the light cast upon her.

"I'm sorry if I woke you, baby," she managed for whichever twin had come to check on her.

"You didn't wake me."

She whipped around, forgetting all about the state of her face just as Hephaestus turned on the light on his side of the bed. The side she tended to roll onto when she was alone. He offered her a small smile and a red travel mug. She knew it was filled with the honeyed tea he always showed up with. She used to think he just picked it up from a gas station self-serve until Dio had asked her if she liked it. It turned out Hephaestus had come to him for this very specific concoction meant to calm the nerves and heal the soul, and ever since, Heph kept a supply in every place she might need it. Like in the kitchen downstairs and one of the shelves in her office at Lush.

Before she could do a thing about it, the sobs tore loose from her lips.

He set the cup down and his cane aside, gingerly climbing onto the mattress and maneuvering himself so that he could sit behind her, his legs on either side of hers. He pulled her back into his chest, and she didn't fight him, turning sideways so that she could bury her face in his neck. He didn't say anything, rubbing her back and cradling her head. Every now and again, he placed a kiss on her temple, and if she weren't coming apart at the seams, she would marvel —again— at how gentle he could be when he wanted to be. Or rather, when he needed to be.

Her fingers curled against his chest, that voice in the back of her head screaming *"you don't deserve this!"* drowned out by the steady beat of his heart. Sometimes, she could pretend it was thrumming out the syllables of her name. Other times, she could swear her own heart was beating out the same pattern.

"Why are you home so early?" she questioned once she could speak again.

He stretched out beneath her, but she couldn't find the strength to lift her head. Then he was holding a handkerchief in front of her face, and she took it gratefully.

"Thought I'd get a quickie in before the next shift started."

She paused in dabbing her eyes to lightly smack his stomach. He chuckled, the arm around her tightening.

"—Actually, Artemis sent me home," he went on after a few beats of silence. "Phobos texted me earlier that Deimos was having trouble sleeping, but they didn't wanna wake you up. Don't worry. I already got them back to bed, but - it was funny to me considering you can barely sleep either. Except it wasn't really funny at all, and it got me thinking about what Hippocrates said, about stability, routine."

*Routine is the key to a fruitful life.*

"And I realized that while I know I'm doing something important, making sure you're safe, I don't have to do it all myself... Well, Artemis pointed that part out really, before she sent me home."

Aphrodite smirked. "Mhmm, I bet."

"But I did realize on my own that I should be home more. I should be with you three, because me being away all the time isn't stability. The boys aren't gonna remember why I was gone when they're older. They'll only remember that I wasn't here when they needed me even though I promised I would be. Plus, they aren't the only ones that need stability. They aren't the only ones recovering."

Her hackles raised on instinct. "Heph, I'm—"

"No, you're not, Aphrodite. You're not fine. And honestly, I'm not either. I almost lost you, and even if you've forgiven me, I'm still trying to forgive myself. And that's okay. Everything that happened was - intense and scary for both of us. But even though I went through it too, I can never truly understand what you were feeling when you were in that car when Orion died or in that house or even in that elevator. And then you just got back up and took in two kids who have their own stuff to work through, and as much as I wanna believe I can patch all that up on my own from the outside, I can't. There are things on the inside that need fixing too, and right now, that's more important."

She could feel it: the anxiety building, the pressure compounding, the panic beginning to take root in and around her heart. And she was prepared to do nothing for it apart from flee in the opposite direction.

"Mm." She hummed, pressing her mouth to his throat and slipping a hand down his belly towards his lap. "You're doing just fine, and so am—"

Hephaestus was not prepared to do any such thing. He took hold of her wrist.

"Nope, not yet."

"Heph..."

"Naw. Come on, we gotta talk about this first."

She pouted, lifting her head so that she could look at him head on. "Daddy... Please."

His jaw tightened, but he didn't release her. Instead, he slid his hand down from her wrist to grip hers and bring it to his chest. Though the steel resolve he had showcased mere moments ago had been diluted by something else, something - softer. Something pleading.

"Come on, 'Dite." It was almost a whisper with the way his voice strained. "Talk to me."

And yet all she could do was stare.

She wanted to. Fates knew she wanted to, but the moment she began to form the words, they coagulated at the back of her throat, and she didn't have the strength to choke them down or spit them up. She was at the mercy of her own mind, and the only other way it knew how to cope was to sit in the silence until everything else settled.

She tried to pull away from him, to get out of that bed and escape the room to somewhere, anywhere that would allow her to do so. But

Hephaestus kept his hold. He didn't let her go. He didn't let her flee. He didn't let her do the one thing she was on the verge of accusing him of doing.

At last, she slumped against him, fresh tears rolling down her cheeks. But still, the words refused to comply with her demands, which only frustrated her further.

"—I never told you I was sorry." She listened to his words vibrate in his chest, confusion coloring her face amidst the turmoil, but she couldn't respond. "For how I made you feel before we... you know. I never meant to make you feel small. I just... I didn't want to be like everyone else, kissing your ass all the time, and I'm sure you wanna make a joke right now, but that's the truth."

He brushed a hand through her hair, her eyes falling shut.

"But you... You're an amazing leader and owner and businesswoman. And you are an amazing mother. You're an amazing woman, Aphrodite. That's never not been true, and I've never not known it, and I'm sorry I ever made you believe otherwise, at least where I was concerned, but I'm glad I learned to appreciate it when I did because otherwise, I wouldn't be here with you right now. And I cannot imagine being anywhere else."

"Shut up, Hephaestus," she at last choked out on the edge of a groan, turning her head into his chest.

"I'll shut up when you start talking. Otherwise, I can do this all day."

Despite the claim, he let the quiet come into the room again, kissing the crown of her head as he rubbed her back and played with her fingers. In a matter of minutes, she once again found herself marveling at all the ways he held her together despite being the one person who could tear her apart.

*I love him I love him I love him!*

And she felt ashamed for ever thinking he would run. If nothing else, his pride would pin him to the floor, but she knew there was no need for that. He had protected her when she had given him every reason not to. He had loved her when she couldn't bear to be loved. He had agreed to raise two boys with her mere weeks into their relationship, and he had sat at Demeter's table to make that same vow. With interest.

*"I love her, and I love these boys, and as long as I am breathing, they will not be alone. They will not have to worry or wonder why they were not enough because they are everything to me... I respect you, Demeter. And I will sit at this table each time Aphrodite asks me to and take your little digs, but I am not my uncle. I am not a diplomat, and I owe you nothing outside of the security I provide you and your district."*

By then, Demeter had set down her dessert fork, her mouth hanging open as she stared across the table at him. Phobos and Deimos had just left the room with Hestia, and Aphrodite had already known that was what he was waiting for, but she never could have anticipated how prepared he was when the time came. She should've though, of course.

*"This is my family. These are my boys, and when they are in your house, you will not sit there and speak ill of me or my family —their family — in front of them. Now you did an amazing job raising your girls on your own, and I'm positive that Aphrodite could do this just fine without me, but she will never have to. Because I made a promise to them, to my boys. This family chose me as much as I chose them. And I will not beg for you to believe in me because as long as Aphrodite believes in me, as long as Phobos and Deimos believe in me, what you believe in is entirely irrelevant."*

Aphrodite smiled to herself and snuggled further into his warmth. What an foolish man. A steadfast, beautiful, brave, and foolish man. And he was hers. Bless the fates.

"Sometimes, it feels like I never even left that elevator."

Her voice was so soft that she could hardly believe she had spoken aloud at all, but all it took to confirm it was that briefest pause of his hand in her hair, lasting a split second but speaking volumes in the calm.

"Or that car. Or that house." She shifted closer to him, as close as she could before she continued. "Most nights, all I can hear is that gunshot in the seat beside me. —And, I can see his face clear as day. Not just Acrisius but Orion too, and the moment I close my eyes and I think of him, all that guilt comes flooding back." She gripped his fingers, squeezing them. "And no one ever says Orion wasn't my fault because everyone knows that he was. And that is the heaviest thing I have to carry every single day, but it can never be the only thing. All that good I did could have been so much better if I'd just listened to you, and I know you don't say it anymore, but I also know you want to, and sometimes I wish you would because at least then, we wouldn't have to do this. And you wouldn't have to pretend you're not thinking it."

Her voice broke, and his lips were there again on the top of her head, trying to soothe some of the pain festering within. He must have felt her shaking by now, trembling like a leaf on a branch made for breaking. As if to answer this thought in the affirmative, he wrapped his other arm around her, the steady thrum of his heart like the sun letting her know where the surface was so that she didn't drown looking for an out.

"I wanted to tell you about it," she pushed on, inhaling his scent. "I wanted to be able to tell you the good things at least. —I wanted to tell you how you saved my life, how - how when Acrisius aimed his gun at me, I dropped to one knee just like you showed me, and I shot first. I wanted to tell you how I outsmarted everyone in that house, how I got the upper hand, and I wanted to tell you that - that—" She was crying again. Hard. "I wanted to tell you that I never stopped thinking about you, that I just - wanted to get home to you, and that was it. That was all I wanted. That was the only thing that mattered. And I—"

But she didn't know what else to say, and she wasn't sure she could speak the words anyway.

"It's okay," he said, merciful. "Just get it out. Let me help you carry it, okay?"

She nodded, more so because it was the only thing she was capable of at the moment.

"And I'm proud of you." His voice was more delicate than it had ever been before. "I'm so proud, and I am so grateful you made it back to me. You - you're my whole fucking world, Aphrodite."

"I just - I don't know how."

"How what?"

"How to let someone help."

"And you think I do?"

She snickered, wrapping her arms around his middle. "I've just always done it myself. I don't remember my mother, and my father didn't help. He dictated, and if he couldn't dictate it to you, he beat it into you. And Demeter always thought she was helping, but she was doing a lot of the same things in a different way. Persephone was there, yeah, and Aunt Hestia, but - they were so independent, and I wanted to be too."

"Being independent doesn't mean you don't have help. I mean, you know that. You delegate all the time, and that's not because you're weak. It's because you're busy, right?" She nodded. "So sometimes you're not just - physically busy. Sometimes you're mentally and emotionally busy, and so sometimes that means delegating. And - wait, come here."

Then he was pulling her up with gentle but stern hands, and she allowed him to set her on his lap so that she was straddling him, her hands on his shoulders and his hands on her waist beneath the fabric of the dress shirt she wore. His shirt.

Now she couldn't look away, mesmerized by those stormy grey eyes and that lopsided smile. Despite that smile though, she could see the sincerity written in the dark of his gaze, and she clung to it as he spoke again.

"Look, I know I clowned you a lot about wanting romance and stuff, but I've obviously eaten my words by now, right?" She smiled in spite of herself, and he grinned wider. "Right, so - I'm your partner. At work, at home, and everywhere in between. Even when I'm not there, I am on your team, Aphrodite, and I will tag in with nothing but a word from you. I mean, we're literally raising kids together. If you can trust me with that, you can trust me with anything, right?"

Her fingers picked at the seam of his shirt that ran down his shoulder, her lip held between her teeth. Then she nodded slowly. It wasn't that she doubted the words. Of course she didn't. But she was only just learning how not to hate how right he always was, especially when it was to her benefit.

"I'm sorry."

He cocked an eyebrow. "For what?"

"For thinking you were running away."

His confusion only deepened, and she dropped her eyes. She felt she had to tell him, to be honest to them both because she did need help letting go of a lot of things, and this one idea seemed a good place to start. If she could admit that, what could possibly be scarier?

And he seemed to pick it up quite easily that this was something she needed. He wasn't angry. He wasn't defensive. He simply tightened his hold on her and ducked his head to catch her eyes.

"Why did you think that, Princess?"

She sighed out a shaky breath. "I don't know. I - you're always gone, and I know you're working. I know that, but I just let my brain run away with it because - it's easier. And it's easier to believe you'd run because it's easier to be angry. To blame you instead of blaming myself."

"And what do you have to blame anybody for?'

"For needing you." Her voice rose and immediately broke, but he kept her upright. "For - needing anyone. For being so fucking needy."

"Here's the thing though, Princess. You don't need anyone. You think I honestly believe you couldn't find a way through this on your own if you had to? I know you can, but this is the point. You don't have to. No one should have to. You've done all this on your own most of your life. Raised this district from nothing, raised Eros, kept more than one of my brothers alive and out of some prison, and you've saved so many lives that I know you've probably lost count, but you did that, Aphrodite. You had every reason to be someone else, something else, something ugly. So many people let you down, but you chose to be better than them. Than your father. All on your own."

She wanted to cry again. Or she was. She couldn't tell because her vision was still blurry from the first time.

"You want someone, and that's okay," he whispered. "I'm obviously the last person that's gonna complain about that now."

A watery giggle managed to escape her, and he reached up to cup her face, swiping tears from her cheeks before he brought her down for a tender kiss. His kisses were rarely tender, but each one that was made her heart flutter in a way that seemed almost unfair, like she should pay him something for having the mind to touch her just so.

She kissed him again before resting her forehead against his.

"And maybe right now you need me," he breathed, "and right now, we need each other, but that doesn't make you weak. Haven't you noticed how much easier it is to suffer in silence? Asking for help is so much harder, and actually accepting it? That's a feat."

She shook her head. "Where did they even make you?"

He shrugged. "Probably the back of my dad's car or something. You can ask my parents when my mom finally shows up to dinner."

His chest shook with laughter as she smacked his shoulder. "You are a mess."

"Mm, maybe so. I'll tell you what though. You can need me all you want. I'll be here because I'm not running away. I'll never run away, definitely not from you and those boys. Besides, feels nice to know I'm needed, that - I'm not expendable."

"You are many things, but you are not that... As much as I wish you were sometimes." She lifted her head, placing her hands on either side of his neck. "But - you're the one I was waiting for, and I do need you. I'll always need you, and even if I didn't, I want you here. For good."

"And as long as that's true, I'll be right here, Princess."

She kissed him again, and at last, his hold gave way, allowing her to melt into him. His arms wound around her fully, an act of avid restoration on this crumbling house she called a body. She was crying again, but it no longer felt suffocating. It felt freeing.

It felt like progress.

# 4

## RAISING SPIRITS

### HEPHAESTUS & APHRODITE

The sports arena looked completely different than it had just a few nights ago when Hephaestus and the twins had come to watch the soccer game. Hephaestus watched as tables and chairs and handmade decorations went up all around him. The fact that Apollo had agreed to let them throw a party here during the soccer season was still baffling to Heph if he were being honest, but he wasn't about to complain. After all, this was what the boys had wanted, and usually what the boys wanted, the boys got.

"No, no, over there!" Aphrodite's shrill voice carried across the field. "I want the cake hidden until it's time to cut it!"

Hephaestus wanted to point out that the twins would be blowing candles out before the cake got cut, so it would actually have to come out a few minutes prior, but judging by the shade of red in Aphrodite's face(and the "unfortunate" morning they'd had), he thought better of it. He was trying to get really good at thinking better of things like that.

Besides, once his eyes snagged on her, all of his attention did too.

She looked good. Of course, she looked good. Every single day, she was the most radiant thing he had ever seen, but today, it was in a way he had not anticipated. The casual, comfortable kind of good that made him feel both overdressed and overstimulated. She was in a maroon tracksuit, form fitting by design and absolutely unfair by nature. Her thick hair was tied up, leaving her neck on full display, and if Hephaestus focused, he could still feel her pulse against his lips where it had been pressed last night. The tension in his shoulders dissipated, and when she turned to him, the tension in hers seemed to do the same.

She, Eros, and Dionysos had done most of the planning for today since Heph was still on the mend from falling through the roof of a crumbling building. Whatever they hadn't done, Hecate and Persephone had. They had wanted a way to both raise spirits after everything that had happened during the Blood Moon Banquet. They had also wanted to celebrate the progress of both twins in both school and their individual treatment plans.

When the boys been asked what day they wanted to celebrate their birthdays, Hephaestus had expected them to pick the same day. However, they had each opted to share a day with one of their parents, Phobos with Aphrodite and Deimos with Hephaestus. Though when asked if the party could still be held during the summer as a collective event, they were swift to agree.

Heph hadn't been sure they could pull off such a large event in the time they'd had. It was foolish of him to underestimate Aphrodite's ability —or Dio's for that matter— to put something together extravagant in record time. Add her inability to admit defeat, and there was nothing she could not do.

She loved the twins in the same way — she refused to do anything less than the absolute most. And Hephaestus loved her for that.

Someone called her name, and her attention left him as she went back into party planner mode.

"Does the honeymoon phase ever end for you two?"

Hephaestus scoffed, his head swiveling to look up as Hermes and Dio appeared on either side of his chair.

He grunted and settled back into his seat. "We have never had a honeymoon phase. We aren't built for it."

"Well, you two seem to be doing a great job with everything," Hermes insisted. "And the twins are gonna love this."

"Where are they? I thought you two were bringing them."

"We did," Dio assured him. "They're with Artemis and Apollo checking out the tunnel. Apollo's gonna let them run out of it once everyone gets here."

Hephaestus glanced around. He hadn't noticed how many people were already filing onto the field. Though it wasn't entirely a field at the moment what with the raised platform, the two grand fountains flanking it, and the many miniature replicas of the twins' favorite structures from Apollo's gallery book.

"You know, instead of a birthday, you two could've done something else to break the tension," Dio said coyly, nudging Heph's ribs with his elbow. "Like a wedding."

Heph smirked. "I was under the impression you would be doing that first, Brother."

Dio snorted. "Why would I go first? You have kids, and you and 'Dite have been together longer." Hephaestus only gave him a pointed look, and Dio's resolve quickly deteriorated. "...And Athena and I are taking it slow...er."

"Mhm." Heph sighed. "There is nothing wrong with that, Brother. As for us, we've - already done it all. We can save the wedding for when we inevitably need another pick-me-up, but we're already everything we can possibly be. We can celebrate it anytime."

They had talked about it of course— because Hephaestus had assumed that was the next step although he felt exactly as he explained to Dionysos now—but Aphrodite had (surprisingly) felt the same way. She was content with where they were, how they were, and the celebration itself could be shelved not only for when it was needed but also when they could afford it the time and space it —and they—deserved.

"'Inevitably' is right," Hermes asserted, crossing his arms over his chest. "But I'm still happy for you. Haven't quite figured out how you swung it, but I am happy."

Heph rolled his eyes. Before they fell on Aphrodite again. She was taking a water break with Persephone.

"You know, we argued this morning."

He didn't know why he said it, the confession slipping out easily over relaxed lips. He was over the argument itself, but there was something about the entire thing that he was still hung up on.

"About?" Hermes urged.

Heph shifted in his seat. "About what the boys were gonna wear. I said street clothes were fine because they were definitely gonna get dirty, but Aphrodite was hellbent on putting them in suits."

Dio made what sounded like a choking sound, which was exactly how he'd always felt about suits to Hephaestus's memory. Not that it stopped him from putting one on whenever Athena asked.

"We went at it for half an hour at least," Heph went on. "Standing at two ends of the damn room, throwing those pointless little jabs back and forth. Not - you know, like we used to, but still. Then I don't know. I turn around, and the boys are coming down the stairs, and they're in their brand new baby blue tracksuits, looking fresh out of one of D's nightclubs because they're a bit baggy. We bought 'em big with the kids growing an inch a week and all, and - Phobos says, 'we compromised for you'. And we just could not stop laughing. Because they ended the argument without saying anything at all. Just like that. That simple. They just handled it themselves."

"You've gotta learn to trust your children."

All three brothers turned around to see Charon coming towards them, Hades at his side. It was odd to see the two of them not in suits, or at least a dress shirt, Charon in a white t-shirt and khaki pants of all things and Hades in a lavender polo that complemented his dark skin and black slacks. They hugged each of the brothers in turn.

"They didn't have much choice in anything before they made it to you," Charon went on, placing a hand on Heph's shoulder, "but that doesn't mean they are incapable. It only means they need the freedom to exercise the ability. And all they need from you really is your support."

Hephaestus smiled to himself, thinking back to how Charon always let him decide what project they would be working on each weekend. A weapon, a rack, a vehicle engine; and he also extended the privilege of choosing the toolkit they would use, each of them hand-crafted by Charon himself with different strengths and specialties. To start, Hephaestus picked the wrong one more often than not, and it showed in the work, but Charon never grew upset. He never scolded or scrutinized in a scathing way. He would simply let Heph work out why it didn't work and which would have worked better.

Heph didn't even need to know the full layout of a project to know which toolkit to use now, and he had employed the same process with the boys without thinking twice about it. He supposed extending that to other aspects of their lives was the next step.

"Besides," Charon sighed, pulling him back, "you don't want them thinking they're always gonna have to jump into action when you two argue. It'll do more harm than good. For everyone."

"You're right," Heph agreed. "I - we don't want that."

"And anyway, you and Aphrodite don't always need to make it about the boys, you know," Hades added cautiously. "You two can have disagreements and arguments and - decisions that have nothing to do with them. It doesn't make you bad parents."

"They make us better," Heph said, pushing himself to his feet as more people swept down onto the field from the stands. It was odd for Heph to realize most of them were just family and close friends. It was so rare for them all to be in one place. "But you're right. I don't want our entire relationship to be built on being parents, and I definitely don't want that to be the reason we're trying at all."

"Then don't let it be. You have something very special here. Cherish it for what it is. Those boys will always be the center of the universe for you both, but it doesn't mean you forget yourselves."

"Balance is key," Hermes tacked on with a tone of faux seriousness.

Heph rolled his eyes just as Eros' smooth voice erupted from the speakers all around them. The lights darkened, and above, on the large scoreboard in the center of the field, pictures of the twins filled the screens that encircled it.

"And now...the moment we've all been waiting for... please welcome to the field our birthday boys, your favorite miniature architects and my most beloved baby brothers, Deimos and Phobos!"

Cheers erupted across the space as horns sounded, spotlights shining on the mouth of the tunnel at the opposite end of the field. The first thing Heph saw was the baby blue tracksuit, but soon, Phobos came out full speed, rushing to distribute high fives and hugs wherever they were needed. You would never know he'd had a broken leg just months before. Fates, you wouldn't know he'd stepped out of the underworld just months before.

Deimos was slower coming out, still more shy than his brother but grinning all the same as he ran a hand through his hair. While Phobos preferred to keep his head shaved down, Deimos liked to keep the top longer. Just like his father's.

He hugged both of his grandmothers, who Heph hadn't noticed until just then when he felt Charon stiffen beside him, and then Deimos hugged his mom. He made it all the way to Hephaestus before Phobos was done with his world tour, and he wrapped his arms around Heph's waist, burying his face in his father's shoulder. Soon, he would be too tall to do that comfortably. Heph enveloped him in his arms, cradling his head and trying to savor it for as long as he could. It never got old, being a father. Their father.

"Happy birthday, Son," Heph whispered into his hair.

"It's not our birthday," Deimos muttered.

Heph chuckled. "Yeah, don't tell your mother that. Again." Deimos looked up, his bronze skin catching the last dregs of a setting sun. They smiled at one another. "Besides, that means two sets of gifts this year, and your Grandma Demeter really loves spending the coin, so..."

"Yeah, Aunt Persephone said she bought us bikes."

Hades snorted a laugh. "Of course she did."

"Don't tell Demeter that either," Heph warned, ruffling Deimos's hair. "She might come for us all if we ruin the surprise."

Phobos ran up to them then, stopping just short of bowling his father over. He was growing quickly, stretching out so that he now had an inch on his brother he would never let anyone forget about. He would certainly be taller than Hephaestus and Charon both soon, and Deimos would follow close behind.

Music came on over the speakers as food carts were rolled out, people finding seats at tables after dropping their gifts off near one of the fountains. Heph watched the twins run off when Demeter called them over. Dionysos soon left to meet Athena in the parking lot and unload their gifts, and Hermes and Hades went straight for the food. Charon remained beside Hephaestus, and Heph only gave him a few minutes' reprieve before throwing him a sly smirk.

"Don't start," Charon said softly, not looking at him.

"Start what?" Heph scoffed. "You know you can go talk to her, right, Pop? You already did the hard part."

"What hard part would that be?"

"You two talked at the hospital. Multiple times."

"And what have I told you about talking? Talking is not—"

"—the same as having a conversation," Heph drawled in time with his dad. "So have a conversation then."

"This hardly seems like the venue."

"This is literally the point of the venue. There's always gonna be an excuse, Pop. But the whole point of this party was to start fresh, find peace. And we don't know how long that peace will be left to us, so..."

At last, Charon glanced over at him, his face clear but his jaw tight. Heph knew how badly his father wanted to go up there and talk to Hera. Heph also knew how it pained him each time she grew skittish and slipped out of an encounter prematurely. But she was trying. He knew that. And after everything that had happened this year, good and bad, and everything that had happened before, all he wanted was for his parents to be happy for once. Or again. Whichever they chose to frame it as, he just wanted for them to choose it this time.

Charon seemed to concede as he clapped a hand on Heph's shoulder for a moment before making his way towards where Hera sat with Medusa and Hestia. Laughter filled the air, threading through the baseline of whatever song was playing on Eros's playlist, and that peace they'd been flagging down began to settle across the field. And it was all...family. All of it, every single person there. From Poseidon and Amphitrite to Erebus and Nyx, Achilles and Hector to Nike and Atlanta, these were the people who signified home. Hephaestus had been taking that for granted for a really long time.

When Dio and Athena returned, Hephaestus followed them to the main family table, sitting between Aphrodite and Deimos although Phobos quickly asked her to swap him places. She rolled her eyes but kissed his forehead and obliged regardless, taking his seat beside Demeter for herself. Hephaestus noted that Demeter was actually speaking to Persephone today, like with friendly conversation and not subtle barbs and jabs, despite the fact Hades sat on the other side of her. The elder woman tended to do really well around the twins, and she'd gone from tossing snobbish remarks at Hephaestus any chance she got to a quiet sort of respect. He would take it.

She'd also made friends with Hera and Medusa though, which Aphrodite seemed relieved about. Hestia surely was. Demeter had never been one for friends, but given the stories Heph had heard about Persephone's father and his family, he could understand. He'd protected himself with standoffish isolation as well because of Zeus, and her ex-husband sounded fully prepared to give Zeus a run for his money.

"Aunt Medusa, do we get our present tonight?" Phobos staged whispered across the table.

"I think we should wait for daytime," Medusa returned, her smile as easy as always. "When we have prime visibility."

"And what gift is this?" Aphrodite asked. Demeter looked poised to do the same, but Hephaestus focused on his roast.

"Aunt Medusa said we could drive her new car!" Phobos shouted, triumphant.

Hephaestus raised his brows but didn't dare look at what was surely shock on Aphrodite's face. He was going to pretend he hadn't already agreed offhandedly to Medusa's suggestion weeks ago. He instead bumped his shoulder against Phobos' and looked up at Medusa.

"And what kinda new car is it?"

"This year's Gorgon," Medusa explained, a glimmer in her dark eyes. "It's finally received certification and can go into production starting this winter. All the newest features too, of course. Safety is a top priority."

She winked at Hephaestus and Aphrodite, the latter relaxing some and nodding in acquiescence. "Newest features" meant there was auto-drive, and auto-drive meant the boys —mainly Phobos— were less likely to total it and get themselves hurt. Medusa must have gotten this model specifically for the boys to drive because her official racing vehicles did not have that feature. That kind of defeated the purpose of the race. Or at least most of the thrill of one.

"How long do we get each?" Phobos questioned now. "Like a weekend?"

"Like an hour," both Hephaestus and Aphrodite shot back.

"Two hours?" Deimos questioned slowly.

"Let's see how you do with the first one," Medusa said. "And maybe next year, if you manage to get your permits, I will consider a weekend."

"Yeah!"

The twins shouted in unison, and Hephaestus couldn't help but grin. It was just hitting him now, the realization that this was all going so very quickly. The boys were fifteen now, the frail vulnerability they had arrived here with now replaced with vibrant life that refused to go unlived. And the youth that had been snatched from them long before would never be restored to them much less their parents. They had to do what they could with the time they were given.

But Hephaestus wasn't bitter, not as he had been, not anymore. He would still get to teach them to shave. He would get to see them play their first soccer game and graduate and —Fates help him— drive their first racing car. He would get to love them for the rest of his life, and that was more than enough. Most days, it felt like more than he deserved.

Watching them open presents after dinner made today one of those days. Their joy was infectious. He was sure Phobos was going to cry when he opened Apollo's gift, an art kit for his blueprint sketches. Of all the hobbies he'd cycled through in the past few months, he was still resolute about the architecture career.

Deimos got an art kit too, but he must have told Apollo he was becoming a bit more interested in the interior art of a place because rather than the graph paper Phobos received, Deimos got a sketchbook of thick paper and a canvas of gracious size. He was absolutely thrilled.

"How the Fates am I supposed to follow this up?" Hermes groaned.

"You aren't," Apollo returned, cool as ever.

"I will," Dio announced with a grin, and Hermes groaned once more. "Boys, you will be absolutely awed to know that your Uncle Dio —yes, me— has managed to close a deal that ensures next year's soccer national title game will be held right here in this arena."

"WHAT!" The twins were on their feet before Heph knew what was happening, Phobos slapping his palms on the table.

"No way, Uncle D, really!" Deimos was flushed red with his elation.

"Yes way! And you two? The best seats in the house."

"Right next to the field!"

"Boy, I said the best seats. Those are second best. We'll be on the field. The sidelines, to be more specific."

The twins nearly threw the whole table over, and not even Aphrodite scolded them for it, watching as they jumped around and hollered. Okay, so maybe they were still small children in a lot of ways. They still had some time.

After the presents finished up and the twins were riding their bikes around with their school friends, Hephaestus stood watching over the cleanup, making sure the place was spotless. Tired as he was, he felt immeasurably content, thinking of how utterly happy Deimos and Phobos were. And how happy Aphrodite had been. The stress she had been wearing around since he went into the hospital —despite what he'd said to her about carrying so much— had been wearing her down and souring her mood, and he had been so afraid of what it would do to her. To them. To the boys.

They still had their rough moments. She was passionate, and she was fearless, and he loved that about her, but sometimes it would cut, and he would be too damn proud to step back, too damn stubborn to relinquish the last word.

They were learning, getting better, but he didn't want to keep fighting for inches. He wanted to commit to being better to her, for her. For their family. Because he wanted to do this with her again and forever, fall in love and raise kids and make love so late into the morning that they would have to call into work. He wished to do it all. And in no particular order.

"What's that look for?"

His vision focused just as the woman herself appeared before him, her red-painted lips curling upward. His own did the same, moving his cane further to the side before wrapping his free arm around her waist.

"I love you," he whispered, the words spilling out on instinct as his forehead touched hers.

She exhaled a heavy breath, her eyes fluttering shut. "And what was that for?"

"I figured you needed to hear that. You did an amazing job with everything."

"Why are you being—"

"Shhhh."

"What? Uh uh."

She reeled back slightly, doing that thing where she fought because not fighting was a sign of weakness, and she could feel herself growing soft. And he didn't blame her because he'd done that thing where he poked and poked with his arrogant snark until she reacted that morning. He was done poking. He didn't care to be right. He only cared to be with her.

So he didn't back down, moving forward to nuzzle his nose against hers. There was a brief hesitation before she relaxed against him, wrapping her arms around his neck.

"I'm sorry," she breathed. "For that, and for this morning."

"You have nothing to be sorry for. We did what we do." He retracted just enough to meet her eyes. "And I want us to do something new now."

She inhaled as if to retaliate but slowly exhaled again. "I do too."

"Okay, let's start with me not needing a reason to be sweet to you. And you not settling for less from me. Not that you really do, but you know. It's okay to want more. I'll do what I gotta do to make it happen for you. I just need to know."

She raised a brow. "Okay, I'm not trying to question you because I absolutely agree, but - I know that look. And I know that tone of voice, Heph."

He wet his lips. "What is it then?"

"That's your business voice. Usually that implies we're going to have some huge discussion, and we're gonna do it at dinner the next day so we can be alone, and I'm going to be -" She bit down on her tongue, the muscles of her jaw tensing. She still struggled to let him in sometimes, to say exactly what it was she was feeling despite her pride. He waited. "I'm just gonna be anxious until then."

He shook his head. "You don't have to be because there is no huge discussion." He reeled her in further. "And I was not trying to use my 'business' voice. I just... I realized today that this is all gonna rush by. And even when—*if* we have more kids, I don't wanna waste what time we have being petty to you. And I don't want the kids to think they have to jump in when we argue. I know sometimes we won't be able to help it. I'm still gonna be an arrogant bastard, and you're still gonna be a pain in the ass, and that's who I fell in love with, so I'm not complaining, but we can find a balance."

She tried to fight a smile and failed. "You think you're slick."

"Oh, I know I am." His smile widened as he brushed a hand over her cheek. "And all I need you to know is that I do not love you any less today than I did the first time I said it. And I do not love you more just because we're raising kids together. How I feel about you is... it's independent from all else. For the most part."

"What do you mean 'for the most part'?"

His lips twitched. "I mean - I do feel some type of way watching you with them. I admire the hell out of you, and I love getting to see you be a mother to our kids, but - even if we didn't have kids yet, I would still love you the way I do now. I would still wanna be with you."

She swallowed, biting her lip. "So you won't just - stay for the kids?"

"I would never just stay for the kids, Aphrodite. I couldn't. Not that I'd ever up and leave them, but I'm not about to give up on you either. Not even close. It's because I love you that I was able to be a father in the first place. I could have never committed to this with anyone else. It's you. And it will always be you. This is our family, and I will fight for it every day of my life."

She stared at him for a long moment, saying nothing, but he could tell by the tremble in her lower lip that she understood. And honestly, he finally did too.

Leaning up, she pressed her lips to his, and he did not waste it, pulling her closer until she was flush against him. And every word he'd spoken crystallized between them, strengthening the thread that bound him to her in every way he could be.

"This is a children's party," someone hissed, and Hephaestus need not look up to see it was Dionysos.

Though he supposed it was better than Demeter.

"You're so getting lucky tonight," Aphrodite whispered against his lips when they parted.

"Mm, that was the plan."

Glancing up at him, she softened. "I love you. And I could not imagine doing this with anyone else but you. —As in I never would've just done this for anyone else but you."

"Me either. Never in a million years."

She grinned. "Good."

Kissing her once more, he held her as long as he could, bathing in the warmth of it and clinging to the emotion it bred. *I love you*. He realized then that he had been waiting to hear her say it all day.

# 5

# DEPRIVED

## HADES & PERSEPHONE

OTE: *Despite my best efforts, this story is likely NOT for people who know how deprivation chambers work in real life. Sorry! CW for sensory deprivation.*

SHE COULD HEAR HIM.

Well... Okay, no, she could not hear him. Or see him or smell him or touch him. But she could *feel* him. Or at least his approach, his measured steps reverberating through the space, rippling ever so slightly across the water around her. He walked around the tank with alert caution, a predator circling his prey, and he made sure to step with enough pressure to keep her aware of his whereabouts. She shivered. Her toes curled. It was already starting.

This wasn't the original purpose of the deprivation pod. In fact, Persephone was sure that if Calliope found out they had replaced the salt solution for fresh water and a foam bed, she would give Persephone AND Hades both a lecture that would haunt them for weeks. Then again, the original purpose was to relieve the tension in Persephone's muscles from back-to-back double features each week, and if Hades had anything to say about it, this would certainly serve the same purpose. And considering he was the only one who now had anything to say about it...

The door above her feet opened.

Her heels bumped against the pod's floor as she tugged at the bindings carefully threaded around her wrists, keeping her arms immobile and her head above the shallow water. She lay propped against the small bed —or rather, more like a foam wedge with arms — that ensured she wasn't straining or putting any pressure on her shoulders and biceps. It accounted for the lack of buoyancy faced with freshwater, a necessary alternative that not only assured comfort but safety.

If all else failed, there was a button just above where the bindings were secured to the pod's wall. If she hit it, a light came on that would signal to Hades that there was a problem. All of it carefully planned and all of it necessary. She would hate for Hades to have to worry about her head being submerged underwater in the dark with a gag in her mouth while he was working out her tension.

They could have done this in bed of course. Kept the earplugs and the gag and the light little blindfold secured around her face, but the water was crucial. After a few sessions in the pod (*alone*), Persephone could not leave the vision alone. And once she'd voiced the fantasy, Hades had rigged the entire thing to fulfill it, never once needing more than her rattled words for direction. It was like he had drawn the very images out of her mind with a fishing line and brought them to life. He was often doing things like this. She should probably get used to it soon.

What she would not get used to was the anticipation that flooded her when she felt him step down into the pool before her. It only intensified with the sound of the lightswitch, the faint blue glow outlining her blindfold immediately snuffed out.

He was careful not to touch her. Too careful, his hands —or what she assumed were his hands— sweeping through the water in slow patterns, just enough for it to lap against her skin. Just enough for her to wish it was his tongue instead. She bit down on the strip of cloth secured between her teeth, a whimper in the back of her throat that she wasn't sure he couldn't hear. Yes, the water was extremely crucial. And he was using it to its full potential.

The waves gradually made their way further up her body until the water was washing over her breasts. She squirmed in place, each drop like a fingertip teasing her heated skin. He must have heard that thought too because next thing she knew, he was tracing a path down from her neck to her stomach, trailing through the valley of her breasts. His fingers still refused to touch down, but each drip of water that came off of them was matched by the moisture between her thighs. She gasped.

"Relax, Baby."

Her entire body jolted. Although she could not fully hear the words, she was certain that was what he'd said with his mouth mere millimeters from her neck. She would bet money on it. Whether accurate or not, his rich baritone voice touched every inch of her that his hands refused to, the sensations shooting straight down into her core. She was certain a moan had clawed its way out of her lips, but she didn't have half a mind to interrogate it. A fog crept along her thoughts as her lungs stammered through a breath. It wasn't fair. Nothing he did when he had her like this was fair. And that was how she liked it. Even if she hated it.

Then everything went still.

She wasn't sure for how long that stillness endured, but it was certainly too long. He must have been kneeling there staring at her through the dark, wondering what it would take to break her. And stubborn as she could be, Persephone knew —at least now— when to swallow her pride. She knew how to weigh pros and cons, costs and benefits, and Hades wasn't the type of man to hold defeat over her too long anyway. Instead, he was quick to make her forget what she was holding out for in the first place.

She mumbled his name, forgetting the cloth in and over her mouth for a split second until it stifled the word. Frustration ebbed and flowed, eroding her resolve and eating away at her patience. She squirmed again against the foam beneath her, giving the bindings around her wrists a weak tug. When that did nothing, she moved a bit quicker, working up the water until it sloshed over her thighs. It was the smallest reprieve but a reprieve nonetheless, and she wasn't willing to waste it. She needed something, anything to relieve the pressure, to help it from compounding in the pit of her belly until she split at the seams, to—

She inhaled sharply. Hades' hands were gripping her thighs, prying them apart and holding them there. He moved not just in the water but with it, apart of it, a current in a stagnant pool that she wished to be swept up by. One squeeze of her flesh on either side and she was writhing before him, but when she attempted to wrap her legs around him or dig her heels into his back and urge him closer, he adjusted his hold and tightened it around her calves. Her legs were left as immobile as her hands, her pussy spread and only half submerged. She wondered how well his eyes had adjusted to the dark, if he could make it out in the space between them, if he could see how wet she was beyond the water lapping at her skin... The thought only made the yearning worse of course, leaving her overwhelmed and at his mercy.

Soon, Hades' ministrations became a gradual unraveling of every muscle and thread and nerve ending in her body. Every touch was deliberate. Every breath along her skin was targeted. Every splash and push of water had a purpose that it understood intimately. And with each, a new sound bled through the cloth until they all ran together, and Persephone was so far gone that she could not register a thing beyond tension in her belly. She could hardly remember where she was, who she was, how she could possibly exist in the places he wasn't touching, and none of it mattered regardless. There was nothing more to her world than her lover's possessive grip and the calculated use of his environment.

And when he finally transitioned into his next phase of glorious torture, mercy became a thing of the past entirely. Because even with his hard shaft pressed against her slit, her hips bucking and her back arching, there was no relief. There was only an enhanced urgency to find it.

It took her a moment to realize she was screaming his name at the top of her lungs, her breaths quick, and her bindings taut above her head. He did not move an inch even as she did what she could to create friction between them, to grind her clit into the underside of his dick until she came undone all over it, but... Well, he was just out of reach.

He squeezed her legs once more in warning, and she fought to still herself, to find some semblance of self-control that she could chew on, to keep herself focused on something other than her need. If only for a moment. Yet Hades knew her body as well as she did, and to some extent, more so. Therefore, if he wished to rob her of focus, he would, and there was not a thing she could do about it.

Still, she forced her body to relax, judging her rate of success by the slow loosening of his hold. He pulsed against her, the sensation shooting up and down her spine at a rapid pace. Oh, what she would give to see him right now, no doubt kneeling there stoic and steady in his intentions. But his eyes would say it all. They always did, romantic and reverent as they crawled along her body with almost as much pressure as his lips would.

She felt them now, tracking the water droplets that caressed her belly before they slipped off the side of her hip back into the pool. His focus made her focus. She shut her eyes behind the blindfold and set her full attention on those droplets of water and their featherlight kiss. She honed in on them, attempting to draw more of a sensation from their descent, to fill some void or find some small reprieve. She chased it with reckless abandon.

So she wasn't at all prepared when he rammed into her in one fluid motion, a current rushing through the pool, through her.

She bucked her hips with a strangled cry, tugging hard on the ties. Not that it mattered. His forward motion alleviated any chance of proper tension, her body climbing up the foam towards the wall. She was blinded by her own ecstasy, submerged in the pleasure he conjured for her and further constructed with each thrust. She could feel his grunts rumble between them, and she yearned to hear them. She loved when the sound devolved from something curt and composed to something feral and relentless. She loved watching him come apart just to make sure she came first. And no matter how hard she tried —though she was trying quite hard— she could not envision them as they truly were, could not recreate them in her mind in the way they needed to be recreated. Yet she could feel them, and somehow, that was far more effective. Still, the need was so great, she was convinced there was nothing that could sate her. Yet she pleaded for it anyway.

When Hades released her thighs, she was certain that it signaled his complete loss of control, and she would be able to at least wrap her legs around him. But no, instead he took hold of each of her ankles, spreading her legs until her toes touched the walls of the pod. And with that, all hope was lost.

She screamed herself hoarse as water rushed over her, crashing up against the sides of the pad until it felt like rain all around her. Hades leaned forward, shifting his weight and changing trajectory. Her clit glanced off of him, another valve unscrewed so that another current of pleasure could flood her from head to toe. Curses and obscenities alike became a jumble of muffled words neither really cared to decipher. Not that he needed to. He knew damn well what he was doing to her. And he knew he did it well.

Persephone twisted and turned, trying to work free of his grasp or grind down further on his cock or somehow create enough fiction to catch flame so that maybe she would finally be sated. Yet Hades allowed nothing. He slowed down and sped up as he pleased, knocking everything in her loose with two rough strokes before slowing enough to swivel his hips and make her plead to the Fates for rescue. Again and again, he pushed her to the edge only to yank her back from it, the ruthless kind of fuck he once saved for special occasions yet now was the golden standard she worked him up for.

And without being able to hear him or see him or touch him or taste him or shout at him to make her cum —at least coherently— all she could do was lean into the sensation of every filthy thing he was doing to her body with his wicked mouth and strong hands and thick cock. And absent every other possible distraction, that feeling, that indisputable and unmatched euphoria, was something divine.

She did not even notice when he lowered her legs back down, releasing them in favor of taking a firm hold on her waist. There was no more alternating, no more speeding up and slowing down, no more need for begging. There were only his hands on her waist and his thrust quickly and continuously entering her slick folds until the coil in her belly tightened to its limits and there was nothing left to hold her together.

She came with a broken wail, her hips rising completely out of the water and every muscle in her body going taut. He used it to his advantage, continuing to fuck her with more urgent movements. It was evident in the haste and depth of his stroke that her orgasm did as much for him as it did for her. She had no clue how it was that this pod was able to hold him and his hunger, but she would not at all be surprised if it fell apart at any moment. Just like she was.

Despite her exhaustion, her hips continued to roll and jerk, half of their own volition and half of hers. It was his turn to fall apart now.

She wanted him to cum so hard that his shout made her earplugs inadequate. She wanted to feel his roar in her throat.

And Hades didn't disappoint. Of course, he didn't disappoint. With his hands braced on either side of hers against the pod call, he came with the kind of conquering roar that could move a mountain if it so pleased. And it ricocheted around in her belly, setting off every nerve it touched, her second orgasm overtaking her without any type of warning or any shade of mercy.

Her head swam with it all, so much so that she could not be sure what sound she'd made. Or if she'd made a sound at all. All she knew was the buzzing beneath her skin and the relentless tremors that now ravaged her body with insatiable appetites as she convulsed beneath him. And Hades' own body shuddering against her.

She did not remember him reaching up to free her, but she soon found that the only thing left on her person was him and her swim cap. She did not bother to open her eyes once the blindfold was gone though. She merely wrapped her arms around him and held him to her, breathing him in as if it were the first time.

"Did that live up to your expectations?" he grumbled, his mouth brushing her throat.

"Mm, I guess it'll do," she teased with a yawn.

"Oh, yeah? It will do?"

"For now, yes."

She felt him raise his head, and her lips twitched. She assumed he would chide her or tickle her or something else. Like climb right out of the pod and leave her there in the cooling water. But then he was smothering her lips with his, and every other thought was lost to the sheer gratitude she held for just being able to kiss him again.

"It was perfect," she confessed once she broke away, her voice soft.

"I know."

There was a brief pause before she snorted a laugh, her eyes cracking open slightly as she swatted his back.

"The worst thing I ever did was tell you that you weren't arrogant enough," she sighed.

"But you did, and now you have to deal with the consequences."

"...How much of it had to do with what you just did to me?"

"I'd say a good amount. Might've been a bit more gentle at least had you not told me that."

"Then I guess I don't regret it that much."

He smirked. "Yeah, that's what I thought."

He kissed her again, earning a content hum from her.

"Cleaning this is gonna be a pain in the ass, huh?"

"Definitely," he agreed. "But worth it."

"Oh, absolutely worth it. And worth doing it again. Very soon."

"Agreed. Maybe we should - get a separate one for the occasion."

She perked up. "Really?"

"Why not? I know once you find something you like, it becomes part of the routine, so we might as well, right? And that way, Calliope can't get mad at us. Much."

"The odds of me getting you off again before we leave this one have just gone up exponentially."

"Oh really? Let me see what I can do to improve them further then."

Though as his mouth began to descend her neck, she knew she'd already decided she would. Anything to stay a bit longer in this little bubble they'd made their own.

# 6

## A Desperate Measure

### DIONYSOS & ATHENA

He was so close. *They* were so close. Halfway to the door when Athena's phone rang. Again. For the third time in less than twenty minutes.

And they were supposed to be out the door fifteen minutes ago. But for the third time, she picked it up, already apologizing when Dionysos turned around. She said it so quietly, he could only read it on her lips because it was the THIRD TIME.

He tried not to wring his hands, balling them up and putting them behind his back with a small smile, but he couldn't help grinding his teeth together.

"Hello again, Sokrates." She ground hers too.

Sokrates seemed like a nice guy, nice enough to understand that she was clocked out for the night, nice enough to understand she had a puppy dog of a boyfriend waiting patiently halfway to the door to take her upstairs to eat and fuck and rest. But he was also stressed enough not to ask, and Athena was determined enough not to call it out, and Dio was supportive enough not to demand she simply hang up. At least not yet.

But it WAS the third time. And if he didn't force her to have boundaries, she would be up all night tending to other people's problems the way she used to be.

"Yes, we can do that," Athena said, her tone short.

She rolled her eyes, more for Dio's sake than her own, but he appreciated it. Truth be told, he did like watching her work. He didn't come down here to her office just to rush her out of it. He liked watching her talk to people too, the way her mouth enunciated and emphasized every syllable, the faces she pulled now that she was learning not to bury all her emotions, and of course, the acknowledgement she gave him amidst it all because she was still his girlfriend even when she was the leader of Olympus. And he grinned because he still adored her even when he was slightly annoyed.

Plus, he knew how important this particular project was. Sokrates was one of the representatives for Thassos taking full advantage of Hades' offer of aid, and Athena had agreed to be head liaison while Hades was away in Messara, his first business trip as leader. Well, other than the one he'd been forced to take to keep Dionysos off the literal chopping block in Thassos.

It was wild to think that it had only been a few months since Pallas had taken him hostage and nearly killed him, but all things considered, Dio thought he'd come to terms with it pretty well. He still had to talk with Hippocrates once a week for the foreseeable future at Athena's and Hades' request —well, Hades' request, Athena's demand — but he found that he actually enjoyed being able to talk about the things he thought he was supposed to bury. It was... well, therapeutic.

He perked up again when he heard Athena giving her goodbyes, adding that she would be unavailable for the rest of the night. He still got overly excited knowing he would have some time with her before bed, and he doubted that would ever change.

"Okay," she sighed after hanging up. "I'm turning this off. I promise. Let me just—"

She swiped her finger across the screen. Just as it started ringing. Again.

Their eyes met, both blown wide, but Dionysos wasn't entirely sure just how bad it was until Demeter's voice burst through air, quick and cutting. *Complaining.*

Because of course she was complaining, not even caring that Athena hadn't actually answered, going on about some conflict on the new border between their districts. One of at least fifteen conflicts she'd conflated and reported to Athena in the last few days. Dio had missed many of the details in the other calls even when he happened to be in the room for them, allowing himself to get distracted by a game on his phone or some video he found on the socials. It would only annoy him to watch her purposefully stress Athena out.

But that would not do anymore. They had already missed their dinner reservation, and that was all fine and well. Dio always had a backup plan in the event Athena got caught up at work, so the food had already been delivered, but this was hardly work. This was Persephone's mama blowing up Athena's phone knowing she was too proud not to answer. And he'd be damned if he was gonna let Demeter of all people make his girl miss a meal.

But food alone wasn't gonna get her off this phone.

"Demeter, listen, can we just—"

Cut off again. Another roll of her eyes, for her sake this time, her nails digging into the desk surface. That was how quickly Demeter always managed to get under her skin. Fates, under anyone's skin. Except one person, and Dio had half a mind to call her. To snitch to his Aunt Persephone and ask her to remind Demeter that Athena was not her personal assistant, but he didn't have the patience for all that. For now, he'd handle this his way.

He made his way around the edge of the room, his eyes on Athena, Athena's eyes on the ceiling. He knew she felt bad for making him wait, but he wasn't mad at her. He knew who he fell in love with. He was simply sick of other people taking advantage of it.

"Look, we agreed that the street itself would act as the border, meaning everything on this side remains part of Olympus by default. However, we also agreed to give all business owners the chance to maintain their residency and permits in Olympus if—"

Another piercing shout severed the sentiment. Athena dropped down against the desk as he came up behind her, resting her head against her forearm, Demeter's vitriol bleeding all over the quiet. Dio assumed Athena hadn't done it on purpose, positioned herself so perfectly, but it was perfect just the same. Biting his lip, he ran his hands along her thighs, up and then across her bent waist.

He heard the soft gasp of realization, the breath catching in her throat, but she didn't get up. She didn't look back at him. He wondered if she even could. He stepped closer, close enough to press his hips against hers so that she had to turn her head away from the phone to keep Demeter from hearing the grunt he knocked loose from her teeth. One solid grind, a firm grip on her waist, and a curse followed under her breath.

"Hang it up," he growled, low in his throat. "Now."

But she was stubborn. She would always be stubborn, and it would always stoke the flame forever burning in the pit of his belly for her. She clenched her thighs, biting down on her forearm until Demeter demanded a response.

"No, Demeter, we - gave them six months." She spat out as if the words were some barbed thing latched onto her tongue. "We told them—"

Another disrespectful dismissal. Another tangent. Another hard roll of his hips against hers as he unbuttoned his trousers. She bucked her own hips back, perhaps instinctively, perhaps insistently, but either way, he was at attention from one breath to the next, hardening against her, a hiss escaping him as he was reminded that even then, she was very much in control. She may have not held all of it physically, but mentally? He was putty in her hands. Always.

It didn't mean he was gonna back down.

He pressed one hand into the valley between her shoulder blades, impressed by the fact she was still trying to talk. She fumbled to string words together, even once she reached out to grip the edge of the desk. His hand slid up higher, adding more pressure, leaning his large body over hers. And when she tried to speak again, he rutted his hips hard against hers.

"Oh - I... No, no, Demeter, I'm not - I have..."

He could hear the elder woman now too, but he did not have enough attention to spare her, so he could not make out a single word. Probably for the best too. He bent his head, gripping Athena's neck and whispering in the ear that didn't have a phone pressed to it.

"Unless you want her to hear every dirty thing I'm about to do to you on this desk, I suggest you hang..." A roll of his hips. "It..." A squeeze of her neck. "Up."

She turned her head. Just enough for him to see the challenge in her eyes. Just enough to hear her harsh whisper.

"You wouldn't dare."

He smirked.

Demeter screeched her name through the phone just as she muffled his name in her palm. Dio reached beneath her, undoing her trousers before taking hold of the back of them and yanking them down none too gently. In fact, he made sure that his nails scraped over her ass, leaving a trail of red in their wake.

"Demeter, I really have to go." Her voice was a shell of itself, hollow and strained against her teeth. "We can discuss this tomorrow, but I—"

"I do not want to discuss this tomorrow!" Dionysos heard Demeter loud and clear this time. "I want to be able to go to bed without worrying about this very minuscule problem you seem unwilling to solve!"

He wanted to point out that if it were a minuscule problem, it could probably wait until tomorrow, but he suppressed the urge by tugging Athena's hair back and out of the way and fusing his mouth to her throat. A snarl of frustration was thrown over her shoulder, and if he had the mind, he would laugh. He would laugh at the entire situation and the fact that Demeter would be absolutely scandalized if she knew what was taking place on the other end of the phone —although she probably still would not hang up, and if she did, it would only be to call Persephone and complain further about their etiquette. Not that it would do her any good. If complaining to Persephone ever turned out well, she wouldn't be calling Athena in the first place.

But all these thoughts were lost to a dense fog with so little fabric between them, the front of his boxers damp with precum and the thin lace of her underwear hardly a barrier at all.

"Hang it up," he said again, so far away from the room yet entirely engaged in this moment. This sounded more like a plea than a command. And so did the next. "Hang it up, hang it - up."

Her fingers were in his hair although he could not make out how. "Just - a second."

He was fully convinced she was getting as much out of this as he was. Otherwise, she would have either stopped him or hung up the damn phone by now.

Fates, he loved her.

"I'll give you ten."

Demeter asked a question he did not catch. Athena attempted an answer he did not care for. He counted softly in her ear, his tongue assaulting its shell.

"One...Two..." He reached down between them again, curling his fingers into the top of her panties. "Three...Four..." He pulled them upward, moving them around to create friction between her thighs, against her clit. The pound of her fist against the surface of the desk let him know he was successful.

"No - Demeter, I am — I - am frustrated because I - I have something else I urgently need to—"

"...Five...Six..." Releasing her panties for the moment, he worked his boxers down his thighs until his dick was free. Her hips jerked as it fell heavy against her ass, settling into the seam with ease. "Seven...Eight..."

"Demeter, I have to go. I have to." She was talking fast now, almost begging, but Demeter was talking faster. "Please, I will - call you first thing in the—"

Dio tore Athena's panties away, the satisfying sound of fabric ripping now filling the air. He didn't tear them completely, but one side was no longer connected, so they unceremoniously descended her legs to pool around her ankles with her trousers. He watched them fall, and in doing so, caught the moment her toes curled against the carpet within the fabric of her socks. Her shoes lay discarded beneath the desk, the initial sign of her earlier fatigue.

He dropped down into a squat without thinking. He felt her scramble to follow his path, her hand finding his hair again, but he was already burying his face in her pussy from the back, licking and sucking her lips with unmatched hunger. And all she could do was pull and yank and urge him deeper as she rose up on her tiptoes before promptly pitching herself forward against the desk with a sharp inhale.

Tattered moans escaped her, her head once more pressed into her forearm, Demeter's voice miles away for them both. The lewd sounds of his ministrations wafted through the air, his tongue working her over thoroughly until her inner thighs were slick with arousal.

"If - if you want them, you ask them, Demeter, but I - I won't force anyone out of their home - district. I'm - I'm—"

A fresh growl of frustration rose in Dio's throat, and he shoved himself to his feet so fast that he nearly lost his balance. His palms slapped against the desk as he bent over her, his mouth wet with her and her taste thick on his lips. He licked them sloppily before reaching between them again and taking hold of his pulsing shaft.

Athena's voice quickened. "No, you know what? I have to go, Demeter. I am done - for the night, and I am not going to - let you keep me on the phone for something that can be handled in the morning and can obviously not - be figured out without speaking to them."

But again, she made the mistake of giving Demeter time to respond.

Dionysos did not.

"FUCK!"

Athena's shout filled the room as he slammed into her with a raw grunt, drowning out whatever Demeter was saying and no doubt pissing her off further in the process. Good. He didn't give anyone time to do anything else, gripping Athena's shoulder with one hand and her hip with the other before he began his rough and ruthless stroke, hitting his stride quick and keeping it consistent. Or at least consistently chaotic, which was the only way he knew how to do much of anything. Athena fumbled with the phone, catching it midair as it slipped from her fingers, Demeter's voice now shrill.

"GOOD NIGHT, DEMETER!"

He wasn't entirely sure she hung up, but before he could even think about double checking, she had launched the phone across the room onto the couch. She then hooked both hands around the edge of the desk, holding on for dear life as Dio both pulled her hips into his and rammed his hips into hers. The two clapped together, loud and assertive, a raunchy baseline beneath her growing moans.

"Fuck, D! I can't - believe you!"

"I - warned you," he growled, instinctively whipping his hand over her ass and receiving a delicious howl in return. "I told you to hang up."

"Mm, and I didn't," she managed, peeking back at him through hooded eyes, her mouth hung open. She looked fucking devastating.

"No." He swung his hips with more force, nearly pulling all the way out before thrusting back in. He should have known he was in for it then. "You didn't."

"Then punish me, Big Guy. Real - good."

Not that he needed the fucking help, but oh, did it have the desired effect. His mind blanked momentarily, tremors running up his spine until it went rigid, his hips falling into a firm yet stuttered motion. He was short circuiting right there, mid-stroke, and all because she knew exactly what to say.

He slowed just long enough to regain control, pulling back from the edge he'd been teetering upon. And once he did, his thrust was once more unforgiving, each one driven by the max amount of force he could put behind it. Vicious, merciless, determined, devoted. Her screams filled the office, and his did too. He pinned her to the desk none too gently, his knee crashing against the drawers on one side. He felt none of that, only the intermittent squeeze of her walls around him and the sheer euphoria of being inside of her altogether.

The song they sung together climbed in volume, seeping into the walls and no doubt into the hall beyond. Not that he cared. Not that either of them cared, not anymore. People may still call, but they had long since stopped coming upstairs after sundown without a warning. They knew it wasn't safe, a lesson learned the hard way by both Ares and Artemis on separate occasions. And even if someone else thought to test that, Dio wasn't about to stop. It felt too damn good.

"D! Oh - Fates! Fuck! Yes! Yes, Baby!"

It only spurred him on, already so close to cumming that he couldn't stop if he tried. He was riding the adrenaline, the thrill he'd gotten from interrupting her call melded with the ache he'd been nursing all day, waiting for the moment they made it back upstairs.

He grabbed and clawed at her as she did the same to him, none of her close enough, none of him deep enough. They were both trying to rectify that. He gripped the back of her thigh, hoisting her leg up so her knee rested on the desk. It left her spread open further for him, stretching around his cock even as her walls clamped down around the tip at the top of his stroke.

And the feeling was divine.

"Fuck, Athena! Fuck, I..."

He all but laid over her, winding his arms around her, holding her to him as each thrust grew more desperate. Once again, she was reaching back, yanking on his hair, a slew of curses spilling out onto the desk from both of them. He didn't know when the spark finally caught, couldn't pinpoint the moment that every nerve was overwhelmed with a fathomless euphoria, that the bomb went off in his belly and the coil cracked apart, but he felt it all.

He roared out as his back bowed, head thrown back and face to the ceiling. He gripped her shoulders and held her in place for a final series of short and sporadic thrusts. His thighs were shaking so hard that he was only vaguely aware when Athena's started shaking too, her hips bouncing up and down on the desk as their orgasms took the breath out of them. Until they collapsed in a pile atop the wood, nothing left but their labored pants and the haze of lust around them.

He let the silence linger until his lungs had recovered.

"Are you sure you hung up?" he asked.

Athena went still, and he followed suit on instinct. "... I don't hear her yelling."

He snickered. "Not anymore."

She shrugged. "Oh, well. If I didn't, there isn't much I can do now, is there?"

"No, not really."

"But I am inclined to stay in bed a little later than usual tomorrow morning so we can do this again. I think you've earned that."

He lifted his head slightly. "Why do we have to wait til morning?"

"I never said anything about waiting." She turned enough to reach back and bring his head down, pressing her lips to his. "I'm damn sure not done with you tonight. I've just decided I want it in the morning too. Is that alright with you, Big Guy?"

He shuddered, biting his lip. "You know damn well it is."

"Mm, I thought so."

"But first..." He slowly pushed himself up, simultaneously pulling out of her. They both moaned in response, and he lightly swatted her ass. "Come on. You gotta eat. You'll need the strength."

She lifted herself up on shaky arms. He helped right her. "I'm gonna hold you to that."

"Can't wait."

"And if ever I need help getting off the phone, I know who to go to."

He rolled his eyes as he pulled up his pants before leaning forward and kissing her cheek. "You better not be goin' to nobody else."

"I would never."

Once they finished dressing, they headed for the door once again. This time, Athena stopped first, halfway there. Dio looked around at her, confused. She was staring at the phone on the couch.

"I-" He froze. She gave him a smile. "I'm gonna leave that there for tonight."

He breathed out. "Thank the Fates."

Because it was gonna be a long night, and she didn't need the distraction. He would make sure she had her hands full regardless.

# 7

# DATE NIGHT

## HEPHAESTUS & APHRODITE

The house was quiet in a way Hephaestus could never remember it being, a reminder that he'd never lived in this house without a full family. It wasn't a complaint. The silence was as soothing as it was unsettling, and judging by her demeanor, Aphrodite was feeling the same.

Usually, at this hour, the twins were done studying, and they were either in the den playing video games or racing up and down the stairs shooting each other with foam dart guns that Dionysos had snuck into their possession despite the warnings of their parents. Eros, who had moved back home at least part-time on Aphrodite's insistence —both he and Heph theorized it was because she wanted the complete experience of a full house of family she'd never had growing up, and neither of them were eager to rob her of it— would be in the kitchen trying out recipes while Psyche, who also seemed to live here part-time, studied at the counter.

However tonight, Eros and Psyche had taken the twins to the fair in Atlantis. It was their second time going this week, but Heph and Aphrodite had agreed it was an acceptable reward for the two finishing their school term. Of course, he had expected for them to ask for something that required more legwork on his or 'Dite's part like a helicopter ride or a trip to Apollo's new theatre in Deucalion Heights, so the fair was definitely a welcome surprise. Eros and Psyche offering to take them so Heph and Aphrodite could have a date night was just icing on the cake.

"You sure you didn't wanna go out to eat?" Heph asked one more time as he followed Aphrodite into the house, the takeout bags clutched in his hand.

"What's the point of having peace and quiet if we're gonna go out, right?" Aphrodite threw back over her shoulder.

He smirked. Aphrodite loved chaos, meaning she loved going out, so while he wouldn't point it out for her sake, he knew damn well she was staying in for him. And he was very appreciative. How she managed to love it so much despite spending eight hours in the club was beyond him, but he would probably never share that sentiment, no matter how much time he spent in and around Lush.

"Why? Did you wanna go out?" she asked, peeking over at him with a look that told him his theory was correct. "Because we can if you want to."

"Naw, naw. I don't wanna waste the peace either."

As much as he loved his kids and his job, it was all still an adjustment after years of solitude. He needed the break every now and then.

Setting the bags on the coffee table in the living room, he sighed. "Besides, I think we've been eating out way too much."

"Really? Because I'd say you haven't been eating out enough lately."

He caught the edge of her smug smile as she turned towards the hallway, looking far too proud of herself. He moved with intention, catching her around the waist just before she turned the corner. She gasped as he pinned her front to the wall, his cane dropping to the ground and his hands gripping hers.

"What was that?"

His voice was low and thick against her ear, and her hips pushed back into his on instinct.

"Say it again, Princess. Don't get shy on me now."

"I said—" she gritted out. "You haven't been eating out enough lately, daddy."

She tried to take advantage of it, to turn the tables in her favor. She always did. It was why they'd never gotten along in the beginning, and now it was one of the most intriguing things about her to him. Though at the moment, he was prepared for it and not at all interested in allowing her to. So when she ground her hips back into him, he merely pinned them into place against the wall.

"Mm, well, maybe after dinner, if I'm not too full, I might be in the mood for dessert."

He concluded this with a deep exhale before abruptly disengaging, picking up his cane, and heading back to the living room. He could hear her scoff behind him, but he didn't turn around. It would work in his favor later.

Once she'd changed and settled on the couch beside him, he put on a movie, and the two tucked into the meal they ordered from a restaurant a few blocks away. They made idle conversation about things that weren't work, and once they finished eating, she rested her feet in his lap and he rubbed her legs.

Every now and again, they would both receive a picture or video message from the kids — Phobos and Psyche on a water ride, Deimos trying to win a prize by shooting water into a chimera's mouth with a water shotgun, Eros with a mouth full of cake, and even one of Poseidon and the twins. Hephaestus realized after the second one how much he missed them and how much he was grateful for having someone —much less so many of them— to miss.

"Me too."

He turned to look at Aphrodite, who had the same wistful gaze in her eyes. It imprinted on him somewhere bone deep.

It was wild to see how much the both of them had changed, not just since their talk at the twins' birthday party but in general. How the spiteful and petty people they had been were now buried beneath two loving parents who would do anything for their family, anything for each other. And he wondered, to his own surprise, if anything was impossible anymore after they had done so many impossible things together. And, even if some things were still impossible, if she would try to do them with him anyway.

He took her hand and kissed her knuckles with a grateful smile. He wanted to tell her then, that they should do it again, that they should make their family bigger. But he decided there would be time for that later. Besides, it could just be the peace and quiet talking. He should probably not make decisions like that until the house was full of rowdy teenagers and young adults again.

For now, he leaned over, capturing her lips with his in a searing kiss. Her reaction was instantaneous, winding her arms around him and pulling him on top of her as she leaned back against the arm of the couch, spreading her legs apart to make room for his form.

"Mm, still hungry then?" she purred when his mouth moved to scale down her neck.

"Working up an appetite as speak," he mumbled.

His teeth scraped along her throat, her hum of approval passing through him like an electric current. If he weren't preoccupied, he'd be in awe of just how much deeper he'd fallen in love with her since yesterday. Fates, since just this morning. Instead, he touched her like it, made it manifest into something physical they could both feel. He glided his hands up her thighs and her sides, sliding along her back until he could cradle her in his arms as he continued to kiss her neck. Her hands grabbed at his shirt with a growing urgency, intermittent hums becoming heavy pants, fingers along his back becoming sharp nails that tried with no small effort to get to his skin through his shirt.

Reluctantly pulling back, he relieved himself —and her by the look on her face— of the impeding item, tossing it on the floor. She didn't wait for further prompting, pulling off her own sheer nightshirt he'd been trying to ignore all through dinner since it left so little to the imagination. He took it from her and let it join his before going for her panties.

"Alright, I'm famished," he huffed.

To his surprise, she erupted in a fit of laughter, slapping a hand over her mouth but failing to stifle much of anything. He paused in his task, giving her a curious look.

"Why are you laughing?"

She shook her head, trying to compose herself. When she finally pulled her hand away though, it was Hephaestus who had to take a moment to remember how to breathe. She looked so fucking gorgeous, russet locks fanned out around her flushed face, her red painted lips swollen with his kiss, and the laughter still burning in her eyes.

"I just really fucking love you," she said, her voice a dreamy sigh, and it was like the words had gone from his mind to her lips. Even so, it touched every nerve in his body, leaving a lasting effect. "And you are so sexy when you look at me like that."

He donned a lopsided grin, unable to help it. "Like what?"

"Like I just said the same thing you were thinking, and you're in awe of it." He chuckled, tickled by the sheer accuracy of it, and she grinned wider. "I'm right, aren't I?"

"Mm, let me show you how right you were."

"Ooh, I like visuals."

"I bet you do. But first..." Getting to his feet, he took up his cane and their shirts before offering her his hand. "Come on."

Her face fell. "Where are we going?"

"The kids gotta come home eventually, and I'm not gonna be

jumping up and running around this house if they do. And I definitely won't have my fill anytime soon."

She bit her lip. "I'll text Eros, let him know not to disturb nobody when they get here."

"That's my girl. Now let's go."

"Yes, daddy."

The look in her eyes alone had him half hard, and once they made the short trip to their bedroom, all bets were off. Aphrodite let out a surprised squeak when Heph pushed her down on the mattress, but she didn't hesitate to toss her phone aside and watch him kick off his shorts with hungry eyes. She was quick to lift her thighs when he took hold of her panties once more, no doubt wanting to prevent him from changing his mind or stopping again. She need not worry though. He wasn't planning on doing anything of the sort.

Tossing her underwear aside, he climbed onto the mattress then descended between her legs, whispering against her inner thighs in between the short trace of his tongue or soft brush of his lips. She arched against the mattress, her hand already finding anchor in his hair as she set one heel between his shoulders.

"Daddy, please." It was little more than a whine, but it did its job.

"Please what, Princess?" he muttered against the flesh just above her clit, anticipation gripping him. "Speak up. I can't hear you."

She writhed and did her best to grind into his mouth, but he matched each movement, keeping her from creating friction.

"Please, Daddy, I need your tongue. I - I need it right now. Please."

"And what will you do for me if I give it to you?"

She let out a wanton sigh, her hand clenching tighter in his hair. "Anything... everything."

He suppressed a shudder. "We'll see."

He reached up to palm her breast, but she took hold of his hand before it landed and pulled it up further, taking two fingers into her mouth and swirling her tongue around them. Heph's hips bucked into the mattress with a grunt before he smothered her clit with his mouth mindlessly. His name echoed through the room as she caught the rhythm before he could recover, grinding and rolling into his jaw until he gave in fully, no longer possessing the will to do a thing else.

His tongue worked her into a quick frenzy, the lewd sounds of his ministrations soon joined by the sweet song of her need as she let his fingers slip from her lips. He returned to the original task, reaching up with the other hand too in order to knead both of her breasts. Each touch was rougher than the last, his hips moving in time with hers against the mattress. And when he slid his tongue into her pussy, he was met with the sharp dig of her claws in his scalp.

"Yes, daddy, please! Don't - fucking stop! I — Oh, fuck!"

Her lower back was entirely off the bed, her feet flat against his shoulders, her toes curling and her hands desperate. He raised up with her, struggling onto his knees and returning his hands to her thighs to hold her in place as he buried his face in her cunt. He could feel her muscles tense around him, her thighs tightening as well. Curse after brilliant curse spilled from her lips. She was on the edge of oblivion, and he was bent on shoving her over it. And all it took was a quick press of his thumb to her clit and the rough curl of his tongue inside her.

"Daddy! Oh my - fuck! Fuck!"

Her nails pierced skin, and her feet kicked at him, but he didn't bow out just yet, licking and sucking as she seized up around him. Her orgasm seemed to build in slow motion, and he held fast to her, keeping her in place even as her body fought the hold of its own accord. He wasn't going to let go.

Her thighs shook against his ears, causing the volume of her cries to fluctuate in quick succession. She peaked with a mess of jumbled words and sounds, ones he soaked up with a sly smile. He didn't wait for her to come down completely before moving on though. He only waited for that sharp inhale of breath when her lungs finally started working again, using the time leading up to it to lap up what arousal he could. Then once her muscles began to relax, he dropped her hips, clinging to that surprise on her face as he pulled her straight onto his swollen cock.

"Daddy!"

The shrill shout was knocked clean out of her with the first thrust, and he savored it beneath his tongue, using it as momentum. She grabbed at him with clumsy hands, her eyes rolling back already, her thighs still trembling in her attempts to secure them around him.

"Anything, right, Princess?" he panted, his hands on either side of her head. "That's what you said. You said you'd do anything for me, didn't you?"

Another vibrant moan left her. "Yes, daddy. Yes! Anything, anything."

She said it over and over until he doubted she knew how to say anything else. Good.

"That's my good girl."

He punctuated it with another sharp stroke that had her all but clawing up the bed. He yanked her back down, his eyes fixed on the space where his shaft disappeared inside of her over and over, each thrust better than the last, Aphrodite making the prettiest sounds to confirm it. He would never grow tired of earning those sounds.

"Fuck, Princess."

He gritted his teeth as he drove into her, already well on his way to being pitched over the edge himself. But she wasn't far behind, her walls clenching around him in an erratic pattern. He lunged forward, laying his body out over hers. She gripped his neck the moment he was in reach, pulling him as close as she could, her hips winding up to meet his. He lost all sense once her teeth clapped shut around his earlobe, his eyes rolling and his mouth falling open. He didn't need anymore help.

Of course, she supplied it anyway.

"Please, Daddy." It was the softest whisper, the last bit of her control dripping off the words to claim the last of his. "Cum for me. Please, I -"

"Fuck!"

His fingers curled into the sheets until they hurt as he careened toward euphoria, fucking her fast and hard to the tune of her endless moans in his ear. He came with a cry that hit several impressive notes, his rhythm lost as his hips shuddered and shook in the grip of his orgasm. Aphrodite's legs weren't faring much better, but they wrapped tightly around him anyway as she came again with a shout she tried to muffle against his shoulder. He could hardly feel it. His whole body was buzzing.

Gradually, they came down, with soft kisses and gentle pets, the nuzzle of noses and tangling of hands. In the quiet that settled around them, Heph shut his eyes, laying soft kisses along her jaw. All that was left now was this innate need to be near her, to feel her and smell her and hear her breathing beneath him.

"You think it'll ever stop feeling like this?" she asked after a long while, brushing her nails along his shoulder.

He didn't skip a beat. "Never. Not with you. Not for me."

He felt her smile against his forehead as she turned towards him, hugging him tighter. He wouldn't say it, at least not right now, but these were his favorite moments, when all her defenses were down. And even as those moments became more abundant, he cherished every single one of them.

"Why?" he asked in spite of himself. "Do you think—"

"No," she interjected, kissing his forehead and quickly quieting him. "Never. Not with you. Not for me."

He smiled. Leaning up, he kissed her lips long and slow before laying back down. She said nothing further, and neither did he. They didn't need to, not right now. The fact was finally setting in. This was still real. And they were gonna be just fine.

# 8

# ROUGH DAY, ROUGH NIGHT

## DIONYSOS & ATHENA

CW: pegging

Dionysos landed on the bed with a grunt, his arms splayed and his long legs still hanging over the side. His clothes lay discarded on the floor a few feet away where he'd hurriedly stripped while Athena disappeared into the closet. He had turned around just as she'd emerged, and she'd put everything behind shoving him down on the mattress. She remained standing, taking him in like an artist would a canvas before bringing their vision to life. He shivered under her gaze. She knew he liked when she took control, his dark eyes filled both with a predator's excitement and a prey's fear. She would make good use of them both.

He screwed his eyes shut the moment her firm hands landed on his thick thighs, sliding upwards at a sluggish pace. He was already dripping precum along his leg, every inch of him at attention upon her descent.

"Further..."

Her voice had a predatory edge to it despite its melodic cadence.

Dionysos did not make her wait, pushing himself further onto the bed until he lay at the center of it, his knees bent and spread apart. More than enough room for her between them.

Dinner felt like it had happened days ago, Athena having knocked back three glasses of whiskey neat before Dio had been able to pry the grievances from her throat. She hated to complain. He knew that, but she was getting better at letting herself feel things, good and bad, and of course, he was eager to field them all. Not without proper outlet attached though.

*"You can take it out on me."*

He'd said it with such nonchalance that she hadn't realized it had landed until idle thoughts turned to filthy fantasies in her mind. Though the fact was that she had already been planning on it, wanting nothing more than to get home and fuck him until she was too tired to think about the day's events. Between talking with Thassos leadership, dealing with some new problem Demeter brought upon herself, and fielding questions from across the Aegean about Zeus's whereabouts, she was exhausted. Just - not exhausted enough. She had more than enough energy to wield on Dio, and she knew he would gladly take every drop.

She climbed onto the mattress, her nails gently scraping along the skin just above his cock. It was hard and twitching, and the sight of it had the ache in her belly growing louder. Her hands slid beneath his legs, drawing them up and pushing his knees towards his chest slightly. He fisted the sheets at his sides.

"Relax," she instructed. He obeyed instantly. "There's my good boy."

"Athena..."

Sweat was already licking along his brow, his bare chest rising and falling at a rapid pace. He had his eyes screwed shut, his lower lip seized between his teeth hard enough to bruise, and Fates, he was so gorgeous. And once he was clenching around her midnight blue strap, there would be nothing more beautiful in all the world.

He groaned as her fingers, coated in lubricant, slid through his cheeks and around his entrance. He tensed up but quickly relaxed, no doubt remembering her earlier command. Still, his jaw was tight, and his chest was too. And as she slowly slid into him, one hand braced against the base of his shaft, the pressure exploded outward in a loud shout.

"That's my good boy," she coaxed, knowing how malleable he became when she used the pet name like bait on a hook rather than a whip on his back. "Take it... There you go, Big Guy..."

Gradually, her fingers encircled his cock until she claimed it in a light grip, massaging the spot just above his balls with her thumb. The head was soon coated in fresh arousal, and she hummed her approval as his legs shook around her. As anticipated, he clenched around the strap, but the moment he eased up again, she buried another inch. And another and another until he was losing his breath. Then she started stroking him.

"Fuck, baby!" he threw his head back, his eyes finally snapping open. "I — oh, Fates, don't stop. Please!"

"You think you can take some more, big guy?"

He nodded, hard and fast. "Yes. Yesyesye— Ah! Fuck!"

Her hips snapped against his, and his back arched off the bed even though he couldn't plant both his feet. One of his thighs remained fixed against her shoulder, the other wrapping around her waist. She squeezed his dick before pumping him faster, synchronizing with the rhythm she was setting with her hips. She was going to make him cum first. And judging by the way his toes were curling and his body was twisting, it would not be long at all.

She would make certain of that.

He came with a broken howl, his hands tearing at the covers below him while his body jolted and shook. She held his cock at an angle that let his seed coat his stomach, her own thighs clenching as she watched him unravel, already slick. He sang for her until his throat went hoarse, his body going limp on the bed.

"My good boy," she whispered.

It was a shame he thought she was done.

All at once, she was letting go of his shaft, bringing his leg across their bodies so that he was almost laying on his side. She reached between them into the harness, turning on the vibrator within. Immediately, it was buzzing hard against her clit, the suction catching hold with ease. She nearly doubled over with the force of it, a loud and long moan escaping her that was soon echoed by Dio when the strap-on started vibrating inside him as well.

She took hold of his thigh with both hands, her nails biting into the skin, and used it to drive into him deeper, harder, faster. It wasn't long until she was unable to keep the rhythm though, breaking it long enough to grind into him and the toy.

"Athena - oh my — Fuck! I'm—"

She could tell already that he was hard again, his hips bucking and jumping in erratic patterns. He twisted and writhed against the mattress, clawing at the sheets, but she kept her grasp on him.

"You said I could take it out on you." Her voice did indeed sound like the crack of a whip now., and his hips jolted in response "So take it, big guy. Come on."

"Ah, fuck! I'm - I'm taking it! I'm—"

He tried to roll onto his stomach, but she yanked him back quickly. All that anger and frustration she had been bottling up all day sunk into her hips, and she hammered them into his with ruthless intent. Again, he was hitting notes that had her aching.

She loved how loud he was, how open and eager he was to please her, how even as he wailed and grabbed a pillow to bite down on with one hand, he still reached back to spread himself open further for her with the other.

"That's! My! Good! Boy!"

Each word punctuated by a punishing thrust, each thrust harder than the last. And she was so close, dangerously so, her orgasm reaching for her and coming up just shy. She leaned over him, slowing to a grind once more, reaching up and gripping his arm, his shoulder. He reached around and slapped her ass before gripping one cheek in his massive hand, knocking her straight over the edge and into euphoria.

"Dio!"

She shook and spasmed atop him, the world tilting sideways and going white as her eyes rolled back. Her name and his echoed through the room, her hips still rutting against his and his hips still rutting against the mattress until at last, her body slumped against him.

The toy was still buzzing amidst their labored breaths as she raised her head high enough to pepper his shoulder and back with kisses. He hummed in contentment, running his hand along her leg as best he could at that angle.

"Did you cum again?" she asked, winding an arm around his chest.

"Mmhm."

"But - are you still hard?"

He paused a moment before nodding. "But that's alright."

"It better be." She leaned up, tugging at his ear with her teeth before she whispered, "So now I can ride you until you really cry for me."

He whimpered. "Fuck me..."

"Gladly." Pushing herself up, she gave his ass one good smack. "Now turn your ass over."

# 9

# NIGHTS LIKE THIS

## HEPHAESTUS & APHRODITE

Prompt: Hephaestus and Aphrodite have A Moment after the kids go to bed

APHRODITE ENTERED the kitchen and exhaled a heavy breath. It was simple instinct to hold it when leaving Deimos' room even if he had not woken up screaming or crying in some time. He was sleeping through the night now, which she was absolutely delighted about not just because it meant Phobos was too but because it meant he was finally starting to heal. They all were.

Hephaestus leaned against the counter with a glass of water in his hand, and he offered it to her when she came to lean on the island directly opposite him. She took it and drank the half that remained, an evening ritual she had only recently realized they had been indulging in for months.

Fates, do not tell her they were already entering *that* stage of marriage. Especially since... they were not actually married yet.

Turning to the faucet, she filled another glass for him. He took it but only drank a bit before setting it down. He had been up in Phobos' room, which was also something new. The twins had been inseparable for over a year, both of them sleeping in Deimos' room every night. It had gotten to the point where Hephaestus would go in to wake them up in the morning only to find they had either pushed their beds together or had fallen asleep huddled in the fort their Uncle Dionysos had helped them build in the corner of the room.

However, the twins had informed Aphrodite and Hephaestus just a month ago that they would like to try sleeping in their own separate rooms. Both parents knew how pivotal this moment was even if the twins hadn't called the family meeting to say so, and within an hour, they had moved Phobos' bed back into his room. A week later, they had upgraded both boys' beds to a larger size for the nights when they felt the need to be together. This was aided by the door that joined their rooms, and for the past two weeks, they had been going to bed and waking up on their own without rousing their parents at all before sunrise.

So each night, rather than check in with both of them at once like they used to, they would each check in on one twin —ask about their day or what the plan was for tomorrow, etc.— then they would switch. It gave the boys a routine as well as time alone with each parent, but it also gave both Aphrodite and Hephaestus prime incentive to be home at a decent hour. Though even if Hephaestus was working nights or Aphrodite had to stay on late, they would take a break at bedtime to come home and see the twins. That was a promise the four of them had made, and thus far, they had kept it.

What Aphrodite had also noticed though was that while they were always getting better at making time for the kids, there were nights where they only saw each other, like really saw each other, for a moment. Sometimes it was spent discussing work or the kids. Other times, it was spent having quick and rough sex before all but rolling over and passing out. Either way, unless they had a scheduled date night, it was difficult to keep up.

Tonight felt like it might go the same way. She was exhausted, and it was obvious he was too. With so much going on in different parts of the city as well as many a foreign delegation coming to see Hades and his work, Hephaestus's schedule was a wreck. It seemed like the more people he hired, the more people he needed, and while she knew he was doing his best to be home, she was more worried about it running him into the ground.

"You ready for bed?" she asked, preparing to seize the fleeting opportunity she was given and at least make out with him like a teenager against this island for a moment.

He stared at her for a moment. Well, longer than a moment. It was at least long enough that she started to feel self-conscious. She wasn't entirely sure why either because she could not read the blank look on his face.

Then at last, he nodded, but it was a slow nod, the kind of nod one gave when they weren't entirely sure that was what they were meant to be doing. Like he hadn't heard her question at all. She raised a brow, but when he nodded more firmly, she shrugged it off and pushed herself off the counter, moving towards the door. She assumed he was following behind her until he spoke.

"Wait a second."

She turned to ask him what he needed, but he was already moving past her into the living room. And then beyond it. She remained where she was, staring down the dark hall after him even once he disappeared inside of her study, but when music began to crawl down towards her, she could no longer wait. Knitting her brows together in consternation, she followed after him.

Hephaestus was hanging his cane on the edge of her desk with one hand when she entered, the other undoing the top buttons of his shirt. His thick curls fell around his ears, casting a shadow along his forehead. He had stopped slicking it back when Deimos seemed to become worn out with doing the same, so now they both wore it wild most days. They were adorable together, but Hephaestus alone? Fates.

She loved this look and all the things that it did to her. She loved how dangerous he looked, like a lightning strike in the distance that still managed to send electricity through her entire body. She loved him.

She was so submerged in these thoughts that she had not noticed him making his way towards her with slow steps. One of her favorite songs climbed up along the walls like vines, making her shiver. "For the Love of You" by the Muses, which was a local group that Terpsichore wrote for and sometimes performed with, had one of those choruses that was both haunting and seductive, their voices pouring from the speakers like fresh honey. It was the song she'd put on the first time she danced for Hephaestus when he asked to know more about her early days at Lush, before she took in Eros and the district became too much to run as a secondary job.

It was also the song she put on when she woke up or went to bed without him. In a way, it was theirs now.

He held out his hand to her. It took her a moment to realize what was happening.

Her lips twitched. "What are you doing?"

Although he tried not to falter, she watched the hard swallow he took down his throat. She wanted to trace the path with her lips.

"I wanna see if these workouts have made me a better dancer at all," he replied.

They were still getting used to this, not always answering with some snarky or petty remark. Or at least not doing so when the matter seemed serious. He was much better at it than her, but they could both admit the bite was still there. Still, she liked this side of him. More than that, she liked allowing herself to love this side of him. And to be able to share this side of herself too.

She smiled for real now. She knew he had been working out more with Athena and even Persephone sometimes (she liked to imagine him half naked and hanging from a silk swing quite often personally). He wanted to be able to run around more with the boys, but she suspected there were other reasons he had not yet felt like sharing too. It didn't matter to her of course. As long as he was happy and didn't feel like he had to change anything about himself. She and the twins already loved him. There was nothing that could make them love him more.

"Okay, but don't try showing me up in my own study," she warned, slipping her hand into his.

"I couldn't if I wanted to."

"I guess we'll see."

Though once he had her in his arms, she could not care less about what they were doing. His cologne was a warm welcome, the soft but firm grip of his hand a safety and solace. He pressed his forehead to hers without prompting, and she nearly lost her breath. How long had they been together now? And yet she still got butterflies in her stomach when she looked into those eyes. Ever the romantic, she was content to see it last forever.

Though she could feel the intermittent shake of his leg, he held himself well, but she was still poised to catch and hold some of the weight if needed. His hand trembled in hers too every now and again, but he merely squeezed hers tighter or curled his fingers into her back.

The song ended, but they continued dancing through the next one. And the next until she lost track. They moved all the way around the room before coming back to the center, Aphrodite fighting the urge to pin him up against the bookcase or one of the walls between her paintings.

He only stepped on her foot a time or two. Once upon a time, it would have been punishable by (a verbal) death, but now, she merely laughed and kissed his lips hard each time. She loved him.

"Thank you."

Their eyes were shut when she said it, her head now resting upon his shoulder.

"For what?" he asked softly.

"For this."

"For being able to dance again?"

She chuckled and shook her head, her lips skating over his neck. "For dancing with me."

She hated to talk about them, her insecurities and fears regarding their relationship that still lingered in the periphery of her mind even now. They had talked about it a lot in the past, and she was working through it. Still, every reminder he offered her that he was here for her and not just the boys was priceless.

"Thank you for dancing with me," he said after a moment. "I'm grateful I get to dance with you. Hopefully, every day as long as I'm breathing."

Her heart skipped a beat, and her breath caught in her throat, the possibilities that followed on the heels of those words swirling around in her head.

Really, she had been thinking about them quite a bit since Hades' and Persephone's engagement. Of course, she had known long before then that she wanted to spend her life with Hephaestus, but she wasn't sure if marriage was something they would be reaching for any time soon. Not that she wouldn't say yes without a moment's hesitation if he asked her to right now (or even a year ago really), but nonetheless. It still felt so surreal. Like she was living someone else's fantasy, and at any moment, they might march in here and snatch it away from her.

She clung to him harder even as she raised her head, speaking more out of fear than anything.

"Are you tryna make this a nightly thing?" she teased lightly.

He shrugged, that slight tilt of his shoulders more pronounced beneath her palm. "I mean, if you wouldn't mind."

She shook her head. "I would absolutely not mind at all."

And if he wanted forever, he had it. He didn't need to ask.

At last, he smiled, moving his hands to cup her face. "I love you."

She would never get tired of hearing that, she feared. "I love you too."

He kissed her with the kind of fervent dedication she had come to hunger for. She had never realized just how tentative his kisses were when they weren't fucking until he started kissing her like this at random moments. Now she understood. This was how he kissed her when his words were not enough, and when he pinned her against the study door, she was reminded that she was. She was enough, and so was he.

# 10

## BOYFRIEND PERKS

### DIONYSOS & ATHENA

Dionysos sat at the edge of the bed with half a smile on his sleepy face watching Athena straighten her pocket square in the mirror. He loved watching her get ready in the morning, her eyes narrowed and scrutinizing, her hands moving across cotton and silk like a pianist's, pragmatic and poised. She got dressed the way she played chess, straightened each garment the way she moved the pieces across the board. And she looked very good doing all of it.

He had been avoiding the calendar for the past week or so, but he was still acutely aware of what day it was. In just days from now, Athena would be on a ferry bound for Deucalion Heights, attending Selene's annual leadership symposium as Khaos Falls' designated representative. She went every year, and this year, with everything that had been going on, it was more important than ever.

But he was still getting used to it, being away from her. You would think after all the time he had already been forced to, he'd be used to it. But no. Once he started waking up to her, it was really difficult to give up that privilege, no matter how temporary it was.

"What?"

Dionysos blinked to find that Athena was looking at him in the mirror, a smirk upon her lips. He managed to widen his smile a bit, shaking the thought away.

"Oh, nothing, just - admiring your handiwork," he replied.

She rolled her eyes playfully. "Hm, you and that flattery."

"Are you complaining?"

"Not at all." She turned, smoothing a hand over her tie. "Actually, speaking of handiwork..."

She moved towards him, and he immediately straightened where he sat, parting his thighs so that she could step between them. She ran her hands up his chest and along his neck.

"Look, I know you love the heat of a deadline bearing down on you, and your procrastination abilities are very impressive."

"Go on..." he hummed, pressing his forehead against hers.

"But I need you to start that laundry so you can be packed *before* we have to leave this time, okay?"

He froze all at once, his heavy lids snapping up as his eyes widened.

"Wait, what?"

She raised a brow. "You need to make sure you are packed before this weekend, okay? We're leaving early on Friday. We have family dinner the night before, so you know that's gonna run late, and there will probably be drinks after, so we—"

"Wait." Dionysos tried to piece it together, but his hope was at war with his logic, and he was not used to working with the latter yet. "So - you want me to go to Deucalion Heights with you?"

It was Athena's turn to look confused now. She reeled back, staring at him hard. And at first, in a moment of panic, he believed —and hoped— she would answer the simpler question which was whether or not he was indeed supposed to be going. But no, while he got better at using his logical mind, she got better at addressing both what he said and what he meant.

"Of course I want you to go," she answered at last with a soft curl of her lips. "I finally have a date to that damned gala, one that is much better with the people skills than I am too."

"But - well after Thassos..."

"I realized we work very well together." She smiled, cupping his cheeks. "But no running off unattended for now, alright?"

"I just - Athena, everyone there... We don't know who... what if people—"

"Dio, the same people who came to your banquet after everything in Thassos are the same people who are going to be at this symposium. A leadership symposium, for leaders, which you are. And beyond that, Selene herself adores you. She replied to me directly when I put in our RVSP that she was excited to see us both and she was glad you were coming."

He blinked again. "You put me on the RSVP?"

She laughed. "Baby, I was always under the impression that you were going with me. I'm sorry I didn't make that clear. Or at least tell you. You know I have a habit of—"

"Handling everything yourself? Yeah I know."

"That's a nice way of putting I have control issues."

He shrugged. "Better you say it than me."

She rolled her eyes again and pinched his cheek, but he merely winked. "So you're coming with me."

"Are you asking?"

"Not at all."

He lit up, his grin pushing her hands further back on his face before he surged forward to smother her mouth with his. His arms wrapped around her, picking her straight up off the ground as he fell back onto the bed.

"Mm, Dio, my suit!" she shrieked, but she was laughing, so he didn't take it too seriously.

"I'll iron it for you," he grunted, turning to lay her down on the bed. "In a bit."

"No, you will not."

"Well, I'll pick you out another one."

"I have to go down to—"

"Just let me go down first."

She burst into a laughter so joyous that Dionysos's stomach did a thousand backflips before his descending mouth reached her neck. His hands were already at her waist, undoing her belt and taking down the zipper of her trousers. He moved further down the bed and took her pants and underwear with him. Her hands quickly went from trying to pull him back up to eagerly shoving him further down, and he adhered with as much haste as his task would allow.

Shoving up her dress shirt, he let his mouth draw a path down to her navel and then across to her hip. His teeth scraped the skin until he could wrap his lips around her clit, his chin sitting against the hem of her panties where they now sat at mid-thigh.

Athena's back arched in the wake of a shuddering gasp, her fingers twisting in his curls as she pulled him closer. Her hips didn't wait for him to set a pace, grinding up against his face in that way he yearned for. She let herself lose control much quicker these days, and he was very grateful. It meant less teasing for both of them.

"D! Fuck!"

He groaned against her folds, dragging his tongue through them before he got up long enough to relieve her of her trousers and panties entirely. As bad as he felt for ruining her wardrobe, he conceded that the only thing he loved more than watching her put a suit on was taking it off of her.

He dropped down again the moment the garments were out of the way, offering no grace period before he was pushing his tongue into her.

Her thighs squeezed around his head, her legs wrapping around his shoulders so that her heels could press into the center of his back. He felt the moment she pulled herself up by his hair into a sitting position, but he merely pushed the top of his head into her to lay her back down. Then he buried his face deeper into her pussy.

"Dionysos..."

She pushed his name out through gritted teeth as if in warning, but Dionysos didn't waver. Reaching up, he pinned her by her biceps to the mattress, holding her in place until he had her screaming his name at the top of her lungs.

Lewd sounds wafted up from where he worked, his thumb soon coming to handle her clit with circular motions while his other hand massaged her breast. Her legs kicked and squeezed, her hips grinding and bucking, the growing tension in her belly palpable above him.

Without warning, her body went absolutely rigid, her nails digging into his scalp and her hips flush against his face so that he could hardly breathe. Not that he minded. He kept working his tongue in and out of her, his fingers speeding up against her clit. Then at last, a loud cry was freed from her throat, saturating the air as her body writhed and jolted beneath him.

Thorough as always, he did not stop until her body went limp on the bed again, her panting moans lingering in the air around them.

He pulled away with a deep kiss to her folds before moving to collapse beside her, his face glistening with the fruits of his labor. She sighed her content, turning into him and throwing her arm across his chest.

"So you really thought I was going to Deucalion Heights without you?" she asked after awhile, drawing circles across his chest.

Dio screwed his eyes shut, a bashful smile on his face. "I just... Well, I promised not to be a distraction while you were working."

"And you can still keep that promise." She leaned up and kissed the underside of his jaw. "But I won't be working the whole time. And again, I could use the help with the crowds."

"But I'm - going as your boyfriend?"

"Is that not what you are?"

She moved with a quickness, climbing up on top of him and straddling his belly. She looked so fucking devastating, her crumpled dress shirt wide open and her tie hanging limp over her shoulders. Somewhere along the way, she'd shrugged out of her jacket as well. He hadn't realized she'd been undressing amidst his dive between her thighs. He wished he could've watched.

Her curls were slightly disheveled and her gaze was smoky, her parted lips swollen from where she had no doubt been biting them. And she looked at him like she was ready to devour him. He wanted to get this picture framed immediately.

"D, of all the problems we've had, none of them have ever been me being ashamed of you," she asserted. "I can admit I got overwhelmed by a lot of your - ways of doing things, but I'd like to think I've come a long way."

He hummed. "Well, that's true. I mean you did let me take you to Lush, and we got to stay for that whole—"

"Oh, I remember." She pinched his nipple playfully, and he hissed.

"If you plan on leaving this house today, I'd cut back on that," he warned.

"Mhm. My point is that yes, I want my boyfriend to go to Deucalion Heights with me not only so that he can get me through this banquet but because I know how much he loves that city, and I'd like to see it through his eyes since I barely got to see any of Messara, and I definitely didn't get to do enough of that in Thassos."

"So preferably with less murder accusations this time," he quipped.

She tilted her head from side to side as if weighing the options. “I mean yeah, but I’m not as picky as I once was, so...”

“Your accelerated character development really turns me on.”

He sat up quickly, hugging her around the waist and pressing his lips to hers once more. She wrapped her arms around his neck, holding him close, her hair brushing along his temples.

“Yeah, alright, I’ll be your date,” he sighed once they parted.

She smirked. “Thank you. I appreciate it.”

“And I’ll even wear a suit.”

“Oh, that part wasn’t up for debate.”

“I know, but I like to make it feel like a choice for my own peace of mind. I also like to showcase my ability to do things without being asked sometimes.”

“I do like those demonstrations.” She kissed him once more before disengaging with a reluctant huff. “But the demonstration I’m most excited to see this week is you doing what I already asked. Which is—”

“Being packed by Friday. I got it.”

“And just to make it easier...” He did not like the mischievous smirk on her face right now, but that quickly changed once she finished. “For every day you’re packed early, you get an hour with me and only this tie in my cabin on the ferry there.”

He perked up immediately. “I’ll be packed by tonight.”

# 11

# GAMES WE PLAY (FLASHBACK)

## DIONYSOS & ATHENA

### DIONYSOS

"How do you play this?"

Dionysos looked down at the chess board Athena sat at, his hands clasped behind his back. He had promised his uncle he would do that every time he felt like touching something he shouldn't, at least until he learned to control it on his own. He could admit he tended to forget it altogether, but he did his best. He would always do his best, especially around Athena's favorite game in the whole world.

Athena looked up at him, her thick brows knitted together as she pushed her curls out of her face. She had obviously been quite concentrated, and he hadn't meant to interrupt her at a critical moment, but he hadn't been able to wait.

*Patience, Dionysos. Waiting is good sometimes.*

Hades' words nipped at his ears like angry birds, but he was focusing too hard on Athena's face to swat them away no matter how much he wanted to.

"It's really hard to explain," she said. At first, he thought that meant she didn't want to explain it which was okay, but then suddenly, there was a glint in her eyes he couldn't interpret. "Here, sit down."

She picked up one of the pieces, and Dionysos leaned over the table to see it even though he could see it pretty well from here. In doing so, he knocked several of the other pieces over.

"Oh! Sorry, Theenie!" he cried, reaching his large arms over the table to pick them up. However, he merely knocked more of them onto the floor. "Oh, ships."

"Dio! Wait!"

She quickly grabbed his hands, causing him to freeze completely. She gave him a pointed look before gently pushing his hands away and picking up the pieces herself. He put his hands in his lap quickly, folding them together and crossing his ankles. It helped to squeeze his legs together —and every other muscle he could really— when he was bouncy.

"So the point of the game is to capture the other person's king," she said, holding up the piece she had originally picked up. The king.

"And how do you do that?" Dio asked.

"Okay, watch this."

Dio watched. He did not look away a single time. He didn't even blink. And he latched onto every word Athena said. However, he still didn't understand much of it, unable to comprehend what her hands were doing or what her mouth was saying, much less at the same time, until he was floundering for any crumb of information he could retain. Those too crumbled in his hands, but he tried anyway. Desperately.

He really wanted to know how to play chess so he could play with Athena more. She spent hours in here on the board. If he could play too, maybe they could spend more of those hours together without him ruining her concentration.

But he wasn't very good at it. Not just the game itself but learning how to play the game. He wasn't even sure he liked this game that much. It wasn't as fun as his video games.

And it was really obvious when Athena grew frustrated even though she tried to hide it which only made him feel worse. Eventually, she stopped trying to show him something about a rook and pushed her chair back.

"We should take a break for the day." Her voice was light but curt. He kinda wished she would just yell at him. He bit his lip and looked down at his hands.

"Sorry, Theenie, I - I just get the words and stuff mixed up."

"It's okay, Dio, it took me a long time to learn too. It's hard." This offered little comfort to him. "Come on. I bet Uncle will be coming to get us for dinner anyway."

But Uncle didn't. In fact, Dio had to wait a whole other HOUR for dinner, and Athena went off to read a book, which Dionysos would not even attempt to emulate. His head hurt, and if anyone else told him one more story about a king or anything of the sort, even if he read it himself, he might cry. So he had gone to his room to play video games until his uncle finally called him down to the dining table.

He felt a little better by the time Hecate brought out dessert, but every time he looked at Athena, his stomach turned. He hated that she would have to continue to play chess by herself. Uncle played with her sometimes, but he was getting busier and busier. Dio couldn't even let her teach him which was actually something she liked to do, sharing all the knowledge she carried around. Dio couldn't imagine not sharing every little fact about things he loved with someone he loved. He wanted her to be able to do the same and share her facts with him.

After dinner, Hades and Dio drove Athena back to Zeus's. On the way back home, Dio decided to take more drastic measures.

"Uncle," he said slowly. "I have to tell you something."

"What is it, son?" Hades asked, his eyes remaining on the road but his face tightening. "What's wrong?"

"Well, I'm very bad at chess."

There was a moment of pause before Hades glanced at him and then back at the road. He opened his mouth, closed it, then opened it again. Dionysos watched, hoping his uncle wouldn't be too disappointed. Not that he ever claimed to be good at it, but Uncle and Athena were, and even Hermes and Hephaestus could manage pretty well, so he felt like he should be too.

"Sorry, Uncle," he went on quickly. "Athena tried to teach me, and I can't get it. I think I'm just kind of a fool, especially because of my hyperactive stuff, and so—"

"Hey, now," Hades quickly interjected.

Then he was pulling into the store on the corner, parking the car at the edge of the lot and turning it off. Then he turned to Dionysos and took his hand.

"Listen to me," he said tenderly. "You are not a fool, Dionysos. Everyone is good at different things. Am I a fool because I can't do math as well as Aunt Hecate?"

Dionysos vigorously shook his head. "You aren't a fool for that, Uncle! You do other stuff!"

"As do you, son." ...*Oh.* Dio got it now. "Athena didn't know anything about gardening until you told her all about yours, did she? And Hephaestus didn't know about all the different herbs that have been used for medicine even though he's much older than you because his skills lie elsewhere. That is what makes us all so special, but it's also how we work so well together. We are each one part of a whole."

"Is the family the whole?"

"Yes, the family is the whole. We help each other because no one can do everything. Not even people whose minds aren't as active as yours. But listen, look how many different things you've learned to do when your attention span allowed it. Look how well you work in a short amount of time once you have the motivation. Your superpowers might work differently, Dio, but they aren't any lesser. They let you do things in ways no one else can."

Dio nodded, suddenly feeling much better, but - it didn't last long. He deflated almost as quickly as he'd brightened up.

"What is it, D?" Hades asked, squeezing his hand.

"But - if I just can't ever learn chess, then that means I can't play with Athena when she spends her noons in there."

Hades smiled, reaching up to brush his other hand through Dio's curls. "Now first of all, I never said it was impossible. You can learn how to do anything, but it will require some extra work. You did not learn gardening in a day. And do you remember how hard it was to find something you enjoyed reading? But once you found those graphic novels, you've never stopped reading even if it isn't as often as Athena. Even if it's not the same things she reads. Things take time... But - do you wanna learn chess because you like it or because Athena does?"

Dionysos bit his lip, his bright eyes shining as he stared at his uncle. "Well... I mean, it looks okay, but - it takes a really long time, and it's slow. And you gotta do a lot of waiting, and I know we said waiting is good sometimes, but - not a lot of times."

Hades' smile spread into a grin before he was full-on laughing. Dio grinned back, all teeth, in a bashful smile before he giggled too.

"Okay, listen," Hades said once he gathered himself. "You do not have to do things you don't like for anyone, Dio. Not anyone, ever. Not even for me. When I make something for dinner, and you don't like it, do I make you eat it?"

Dio shook his head smugly. "Nope."

"And do you think Athena would make you play a game that you hate?"

He paused. “No. She never makes me wear the stuff she likes in dress-up. She lets me pick.”

“Exactly. Because we love each other, and when we love each other, we respect each other and our own choices. Of course, there are some things you should listen to me or your aunt and uncles on because you’re a kid who is still learning about the world, but I will always take your feelings into consideration, and so will Athena. You can like different things or play different games together, Dio. And it’s okay if you don’t spend all your time together, at least not on the same thing. You can do separate things and still be best friends.”

Dio chewed on his lip again, looking down at his lap. Then a thought came to his mind, and he gasped, turning back to his uncle.

“Well, I found this game. I thought it was chess at first, but it wasn’t, but I still liked it. I play it on my game mobile. Do you think - that I could sit with Athena and play my game while she plays hers? I can even wear my headphones so the sound doesn’t bug her.”

Hades’ eyes twinkled. “Well, you have to ask Athena because remember, she deserves to have a choice too. And it’s okay if she wants to play alone, right? Because we all have to have our own time by ourselves when we need it.” Dio nodded although that made him a bit worried. “But if she says yes, that sounds like a wonderful idea.”

Hades pulled him into a hug, and Dio let that calm him. Once he had recovered, the two of them went into the convenience store for ice cream for tomorrow’s dessert before they returned home, Dio already excited to see Athena the next day.

Wasn’t he always?

---

## ATHENA

Athena was struggling to concentrate on the board before her and its many pieces, her eyes drifting across them a dozen times without actually registering where they were in relation to the endgame. She moved the same piece back and forth a few times in hopes that would hone her attention, but it did little more than irritate her further. Then the door opened, and she at least had an excuse to focus elsewhere.

Dionysos walked in, his head down and his eyes on the screen of the mobile gaming console in his hands. He had his favorite pair of large, over-the-ear headphones on as well as a box of something and two bottles under his arm. He came over to the table and was about to set things down around Athena's chess board when he seemed to think better of it, going back to retrieve one of the standing trays and placing it next to the chess table. He fumbled with the items in his hands the entire time, but Athena was too enamored —and quite curious— to say or do anything but stare.

At last, he set down both the bottles and box of what turned out to be juice and fruit snacks before flopping down into the other chair with a deep sigh.

"I got the fruit snacks instead of the chips because Uncle said they're quieter," he stated, not meeting her gaze. "But if you want the chips, I can go get them. I don't mind."

She wanted to tell him she wasn't all that hungry at the moment, but that wasn't what came out of her mouth.

"What are you doing?"

"Huh?" His face fell into one of confusion briefly. Then horror. "Oh, um, playing with you?"

"Playing with me? But - you're on your game thing."

He grinned sheepishly, holding up the handheld screen. "It's a game kinda like chess! You move these cool little circles around! And it's easier!" He seemed to realize he was yelling and quickly pushed his headphones off to hang around his neck. "Sorry. But okay, so Uncle said that I could still play with you even if I'm not good at the same games or if I like other games better, so I asked if I could sit with you and play mine while you play yours, but I forgot he said I have to ask you first. I'm sorry. —Is that okay?"

Athena stared at him for a long while. "Why - why did Uncle tell you that?"

Dio looked down at his lap now, his bashfulness morphing slowly into shame. Athena regretted asking altogether, but before she could change course, he replied.

"Well, I - I asked him if maybe he could teach me chess." Athena's heart sank, but Dio quickly pushed on. "Not because you're a bad teacher, Theenie! You're a really good one! But I'm a really bad student, and - the whole reason I wanted to learn was so I could play with you. But you spent your whole chess time trying to teach me, and that's not fair. I want you to have fun too. And if Uncle taught me, maybe I could be really good so I can play with you like a real game, but Uncle says it will take a long time, so for now, I thought this would be just as fun."

He squirmed in his seat, his round cheeks glossy with sweat, and Athena couldn't help but smile. She had never thought about it like that. She was afraid he didn't like learning from her or that he just hated chess and that he wouldn't want to play with her anymore. She had been agonizing over it since the day before, and she hadn't even sought him out when she arrived to her uncle's that day, instead going straight to the room Hades kept for her to try and practice her teaching routine. It hadn't gone very well obviously, but she really did want to teach him. She loved chess, and she loved Dio, and she wanted to share her favorite game with him.

But this... Well, this was perfect. She still doubted he would stay sitting for very long, but at least he would still be here with her. Because as difficult as he may have made it at times to concentrate, she much rather preferred to have him around especially since she didn't get to see him all the time. She could concentrate when she returned to Zeus's where she spent most of her time in her room anyway. Right now, she wanted to spend time with her best friend.

"I think it will be too," Athena quickly said when remembering she had yet to respond to him. "Thanks, Dio, it is a perfect idea. I'm glad you'll still play with me even if you don't like chess."

"Of course, I will." He grinned at her again, so wide that his eyes were squeezed shut. "But - if you wanted to teach me someday, I'll try again, I promise!"

"I want to! I really do like teaching you. I'm sorry if I seemed mad yesterday. I was, but not at you. I was mad at me because I didn't think I was doing a good job."

"You were! I just need a little extra work. And you can always play this game with me if you want a break from chess." He suddenly gasped. "Or - maybe when we finish games, we can go see the horses by the canal!"

She didn't even wince at the sudden increase in the volume of his voice, her eyes widening with excitement. "I would love to!"

"Sick!" He jumped up in his chair, his knees hitting the table and knocking a few of her chess pieces over. He quickly stopped moving altogether, not reaching to pick them up. "Sorry!"

She kept her smile though, carefully putting them back in place. A thought came to her then. Or rather, an overwhelming urge. Looking up at him, she put her hands together.

"Can we - be done with games early? Just for today? The horses will be out already."

"Okay!" Dionysos was already on his feet, heading for the door at a quick pace. "I'll get our boots!"

She watched him go, her stomach feeling a little weird but the excitement thick at the center of her chest. Yes, chess could certainly wait.

# 12

# A LIFELONG BOND (FLASHBACK)

## HADES & CERBERUS

The world was so loud. And Hades could hear *everything*.

The cars on the street, the people all around, the boats in the harbor. But also the buzzing of insects and the whir of a drill and the booming voice of a merchant somewhere around the corner underlined by the sweet strings of a siren song. It was too much, and today, not even Rhea's warmth could shield him.

He liked watching the boats come in, and most days, he enjoyed the sounds of the harbor. It was the perfect kind of chaos for his sensitive ears so long as they were at its edges, and some days, he didn't even need his headphones. However today was not one of those days. Today, he was positively overwhelmed.

His first day of school had been hard. He had missed his mother most, and his father was still away in Nubia with Uncle Amun and Uncle Taharqa for at least another week, so he had been through a hard cry midday behind the gym. He'd sobbed into his backpack and hadn't told. He didn't want his mother to worry more than she already had about him starting school, and he had promised he would be okay. He would never break a promise to Rhea.

Yet here they were at his favorite place, and he couldn't enjoy it because the day had taken his joy and ferried it far away and out of reach.

"Come on, my sweet boy," Rhea cooed.

She placed a gentle hand on Hades' shoulder, but he kept his head buried in the back of her thigh, feeling more exhausted than ever. He hated that the harbor could not comfort him today. He knew she must have brought him because she could tell he was struggling. His hands hadn't stopped moving, and he kept rubbing them against her arm. She must've known. She always knew. She was a mind reader and a miracle worker, and he was horrible at hiding things from her.

And he *hated* himself for it right now. He wanted his mother to be happy even if he couldn't be.

"I've got a special surprise for you, for getting through the day," she continued, her voice soft as ever. "A very special one."

He wanted to tell her that he hadn't. He hadn't gotten through it without crying even though he'd promised. And then he'd lied to her face when she asked how the day went. He didn't think he deserved a surprise. But he still did not wish to make her sad, so he carefully stepped out from behind her to look at the ship that had just docked. Still, he doubted that there was any anomaly here that would help him now.

But he was wrong. So very wrong for doubting his perfect mother. There before him was the best surprise he could ever imagine.

He was running before he knew his legs had moved.

"Baba!" he screamed, his hands outstretched.

"My big boy!" Aten cried back as he ran too, scooping up his son the moment he was close enough.

Hades wrapped his arms around his father's neck with no intention of ever letting go. Even still at his big age of seven, he was always happier in the arms of his father or the shadow of his mother. More than that, he was happiest when he could be with them most.

"Oh, my boy," Aten said softly in his ear, rubbing his back. He must have known Hades had struggled today too. Of course. His parents always knew. They were the best parents in the world. "I am so sorry I was not here to start your big day, but I did bring you something really special."

"You came home early," Hades acknowledged, burrowing further into his father's neck. "Thank you, Baba."

"Not alone."

He was just about to tell his father he just wanted to go home, but then he heard a round of high-pitched barks as Aten turned around. Looking up, Hades saw one of his father's guards squatting beside a kennel. Carefully, the guard extracted something within. Hades realized that was where the barking was coming from.

He looked at his father in question, twirling one of Aten's curls around his finger. Aten smiled.

"I know you were sad that Bahiti has not had puppies, but his sister had her litter last week, and your Uncle Amun saved one just for you. We will have to write him a letter later, but first..."

Aten carefully set Hades down just as the guard set down a beautiful black pup that looked just like his father's loyal companion, Bahiti. The two stared at one another, neither sure of the other. Though the longer he stared, the more Hades realized what it was his father had said. This was his pup. He was going to have his own loyal partner just like Aten.

"Cerberus," he said softly.

That had been the name he'd picked long ago when he thought he might get a puppy from Bahiti's litter. His father had explained that "these things cannot be forced", and while Hades understood that, he imagined himself having a pup for days on end. Now, it seemed he did.

As soon as he said it, the puppy yipped and pounced forth. Hades' heart skipped a beat, but rather than jump back, he found himself falling to his knees and catching Cerberus in his arms. At once,

Cerberus licked away at his face. Aten and Rhea appeared on either side of them in a second, but Hades did not need to be saved. He... well, he actually liked the feeling!

He giggled and rubbed Cerberus' back the way he would usually do Rhea's arm. He wouldn't tell her, but Cerberus was almost just at good.

Without warning, the day's strain fell away from him, cleansed by Cerberus' eager licks and happy barks. Hades would need to adjust to the sharp sound of the latter, but right now, he didn't care.

Though after a moment, a thought struck him, and he looked up at Aten.

"Can I share him?" he asked. "With Charon and Thana and Hecate?"

Aten smiled. "Oh, no need. I've got some for them as well. We will get them from the ship in a moment."

Hades grinned. He would hate for his dearest friends to be without a puppy. Especially Thanatos. He loved puppies.

"Are you ready to go home now, little one?" Rhea asked.

Hades nodded, getting up and taking her hand in one of his and cradling Cerberus on his shoulder with the other. Cerberus calmed in his arm, resting his head on Hades' shoulder. Hades knew then without a doubt that just like Aten and Bahiti, they would be best friends for life.

# 13

# A SINCERE CELEBRATION

## HADES, PERSEPHONE, & HECATE

CW: threesome, sex toys, double penetration

Persephone leaned against the wall of the elevator with a heavy exhale, the car ascending at the most sluggish pace in its journey up to Casino Asphodel's penthouse. Her heart pounded in her chest, its erratic rhythm echoing in her ears as though it were playing over the speakers above.

You would think this was a first date rather than a well earned reunion with how nervous she was, but after being away from Hades for over a month, she felt the reaction was warranted. In the year they had been together, it was the longest they had been away from each other, and she wasn't at all keen on doing it again any time soon. Or ever.

Luckily for her, this work trip to Deucalion Heights was to be the last, at least for some time. After months of laying the foundation and securing funding in Khaos Falls, the headquarters of Calliope's production company had now fully migrated from the posh upper crust of Deucalion Heights to the legendary lot of Casino Asphodel. This meant Persephone would be able to work from home—in the most literal sense— indefinitely. Of course, she would still be teaching classes at Terpsichore's school every now and again as she'd been doing for the past several months, but that was hardly a commute in comparison to the day-long trip to Deucalion Heights.

Though she had told Hades she would be back that day, she hadn't informed him of when she'd departed in order to preserve some element of surprise. Call her corny or whatever, but there was nothing quite as healing as the way his face lit up when she came into the house, and she wanted to enhance that in any way possible.

So much had changed in the past year, but the important things had stayed the same. Like how attentive and charming and affectionate he was with her and how he could read her so easily, sometimes better than she could read herself. Not to mention all the cool nephews and nieces she had inherited in the process, the community it fostered. She now had a whole family to love on and be loved by without conditions like the ones she was given in her mother's house. Being in love with Hades was the gift that kept on giving, and coming home to him was a dream she never could have conjured on her own.

Fates, she'd missed him. Whether it was playing cards or watching movies or sitting beside each other on the couch while they read, her time with him was invaluable and absolutely her favorite part of any day. If someone would've told her she would be head over heels for anyone, much less the leader of Khaos Falls —granted, that had a much different connotation a year ago— she would have laughed herself into an early grave. Now she laughed at the thought with giddy excitement instead, eager to be back in his arms.

The doors opened into the penthouse, and Persephone was swept into the scent of something cooking entangled with faint traces of Hades' cologne. She dropped her bags by the door just as Hades appeared in the mouth of the hallway, his face lighting up like a theatre stage, and she vaulted over the nearest couch and into his arms. He caught her with a raucous laugh, embracing her tightly as she peppered his face with kisses.

"My beautiful. Sexy. Gorgeous. Amazing. Man."

She punctuated each word with a kiss before resting her forehead against his, closing her eyes and allowing herself to simply inhale him for a moment. She could feel her heart slowing to a more comfortable pace, and she was willing to bet it would soon be in sync with his own.

"I take it you missed me a bit?"

She hummed. "What gave it away?"

"Definitely not you hurdling over a couch." She snorted as he inclined his head and kissed her lips. "I missed you too."

"How much?"

"So much that if I had to fall asleep on a video call one more night, I was going to sail to Deucalion Heights my damn self."

"Aww, you were gonna come for me?"

His smile morphed into a wolfish grin. "Oh, I'm still gonna do that."

She rolled her eyes even as her lips curled and her legs wrapped around him. "Mhm, I'm sure you are."

She kissed him again, pressing her body firmly against his before she was rudely interrupted by the rumble of her stomach. He snickered and pulled back, carrying her towards the kitchen.

"Luckily, I prepared dinner already," he informed her.

"I knew I loved you for a reason."

"Because I keep you fed?"

"In so many ways."

He set her down on the counter before opening the oven and pulling out a roast that smelled absolutely delectable. He fed her several pieces as he shredded the tender meat before serving her a plate complete with potatoes, vegetables, and salad as well. Her eyes traced his forearms as he layered the latter with feta, his face painted in determination. Once he was done, they moved over to the table, and he poured each of them a glass of Dionysos' pomegranate wine as she rehashed her adventure with Calliope.

He listened intently, watching her become increasingly more animated as she finally processed what it all meant. They were bringing the most notable production company in the Aegean back home, something that had been impossible back when Zeus was in charge of things and he had wanted far too much of the profits for himself.

Of Course, neither Persephone nor Hades had known this before, but when Hades had asked Calliope why her headquarters was in Deucalion Heights after Zeus's departure, she had finally felt comfortable enough to come clean. As soon as she did, Hades had been the one to organize funding for the move. He had helped make today possible, and although he could agree that Calliope deserved more justice than that, Calliope herself was more than thrilled. She had been trying to come home much longer than Persephone had been in her company.

Unfortunately, Calliope's tale was a drop in the bucket at this point, and Hades and Persephone now had a running list of transgressions newly exposed to the light that he was actively trying to rectify. With Zeus gone, everyone in town was finally ready to speak their truth and talk about the individual horrors they had suffered at his hand.

Persephone didn't want to think about that right now though, not when she was being spoiled rotten with a delicious dinner and dessert sitting right across the table from her. That was all she wanted now, to jump in bed with her man and not leave for at least the next two days.

As they cleaned up the table, the elevator bell rang, signaling someone's arrival. Persephone, confused since she hadn't heard it being called down in the first place, raised a brow at Hades. Yet he simply continued washing the dishes as though he hadn't heard anything at all. Moments later, the doors slid open to reveal Hecate, her curvy frame draped in a sheer lavender nightgown tied loosely around her waist. And not a thing else.

She did have a red bag slung over her shoulder and something that looked like a toolbox in her hand though. Persephone squealed, immediately rushing forward and enveloping the shorter woman. She had missed her almost as much as she'd missed Hades, and now that Hecate was in front of her, it was impossible to suppress.

"What are you doing here?" Persephone breathed as they parted.

Hecate grinned. "Hades said your trip to Deucalion Heights was overly successful, and he thought you deserved a gift."

Seph quirked a brow. "A gift?"

"Mhmm."

"Okay..." She looked between the two of them, Hades still focused on the sink in front of him as he dried his hands. "Where is it? *What* is it?"

Hecate only grinned wider, holding her arms out. "You're looking at it."

At last, Hades turned to face the two of them, no doubt eager to see Persephone's reaction. She bit her lip, sizing Hecate up with dark eyes. Now that she let herself think about it, it had been a mighty long time since Hecate had joined them in their bed. Too long in fact.

"And - what are those?" Seph gestured to Hecate's luggage.

She jiggled the box in her hand. "For show, not tell." Moving past her, Hecate headed towards the hall that led into the master bedroom. "Hades!"

Persephone turned to him now, but he said nothing, simply stepping forward and sweeping her up in his arms with a profound ease. Her pout did nothing to tempt an explanation, but regardless, her stomach twisted with a growing excitement, toes curling as they moved swiftly down the hall. It was almost scary how easy it was for him to satisfy her. He fulfilled cravings before she knew she had them and replenished her needs before she had a reason to miss them. She feared she might soon become too comfortable beneath the homely haze of his love.

Hecate was already unpacking when Hades deposited Persephone onto the mattress, a vast array of colorful objects laid out on the dresser. Between Hecate's arranging and Hades' undressing, Persephone was unable to focus on any one thing. By the time he let his shaft free, Hecate had three of them on the bedside table in various sizes and colors.

Persephone didn't wait for anymore help, pushing herself up enough to pull her shirt over her head and toss it to the floor. Her pants soon followed, Hades' rumbling chuckle echoing around her. But after all of the things they'd done with one another— to one another—she had no shame left to spare him. Instead, she reached up and shoved her panties in his mouth before dragging him down on top of her.

She managed to get two kisses to his throat before he rolled over, pinning her to the bed with a warning look and a shake of his head. She smirked at the bright teal fabric between his teeth, raising her hips in search of even a moment of friction, but he quickly moved to sit beside her instead. She sat up, fully intent on tackling him once more, but before she could find any leverage, he had gotten a hold on her, picking her up and sitting her down in his lap.

"And here I thought you'd missed me more," she teased, snatching the panties from his mouth and tossing them over his shoulder.

"I did," he shot back, "but I also missed you enough to make this worth your while."

His dick fitted itself into the seam of her ass, a low purr leaving her lips. He pulled her back to his chest, palming her breasts as she reached for the back of his head. She snatched the panties from his mouth on the way, tossing them over his shoulder and smothering his lips with her own.

"Don't get started without me," Hecate's voice rang out.

Persephone pulled away from Hades, resting her head on his shoulder as her eyes sought out the other woman. She nearly choked on her own saliva when they found her.

Hecate had abandoned her nightgown, leaving every inch of her exposed to their gaze. Although she wasn't entirely bare. Leather and nylon bracketed her hips, holding in place an impressively sized neon pink dildo with a curved head. In addition to that, there was something in her hand, something that looked like a remote. In the other hand, she picked up a purple vibrator, the open mouth at the top perfectly shaped to wrap around her clit. Persephone groaned, licking her lips as Hades' strong hands spread her legs further apart on either side of his own.

"Go on Hades," Hecate instructed now, stepping closer to them. "Give the queen her throne."

Before Persephone could speculate about what that might mean, Hades pushed her forward just enough for him to take hold of his shaft. She felt his knuckles along her spine as he stroked it a few times, the sound causing Seph to conclude that he had a bottle of lubricant back there somewhere. Then he wrapped his arm around her waist, lifting her up and positioning her over his lap once more.

She waited with bated breath for her hips to touch down again, and once they did, a sharp whimper emanated from her as she embraced the stretch and immediately ground down into him. She reached down, ravenous, and scraped her nails along the base of his dick, sparking his hips into a quicker pace. Persephone threw her head back against his shoulder with a moan, riding him as fast as the position allowed.

She was far too distracted to notice Hecate fall to her knees before them with a predator's gaze.

Persephone only realized she was surrounded when Hecate's tongue swept up her slit, no doubt catching the underside of Hades' cock in the process if the way his breath stuttered was any indication. She heard it moments before a wail ripped itself free from her throat to ricochet around the room. Her hands sought purchase in every direction, one eventually anchoring in Hades' hair while the other clawed at Hecate's scalp.

Hades and Hecate kept going like that, their movements falling into sync, until they'd lured Persephone into a false sense of security. She reclined against Hades' shoulder with her eyes shut and her thighs wide, enjoying the team effort they were putting out. She didn't register the sudden vibration of the toy with Hades growling every dirty word she yearned to hear into her ear.

"You're doing so well, Babygirl, taking both of us like it's nothing."

Yet "nothing" became something else entirely from one breath to the next. Without warning, Hecate's mouth left her and left her cold, but there was no time to comprehend it much less complain before a harsh vibration was lighting up her folds, her clit being pulled firmly by the toy's suction. At once, she lost all control of her body, her muscles spasming and her thighs jumping. Hades had to grip them in sure hands to pin her in place as Hecate's mouth traveled north to ravish her breasts.

Hecate pushed them both back, forcing them to lie down as she stood between their legs. She clicked a button on the remote in her other hand, and the bulb pressed against her own clit began to buzz loudly, threatening to make her knees buckle. Then she thrusted into Seph, pressing the suctioning toy harder against her, both of them crying out at the intense stimulation. Hades' sounds grew louder as well, his secondhand experience just as jarring. At the very least, it was enough to have him slamming Persephone down on him repeatedly with full force.

"Hades! Oh fuck!"

Seph's face glistened with sweat, her hands unsure of what to do or who to grab or whether or not to stop one or beg for more of the other. No one, least of all her, was surprised when she was the first to cum, a shrill scream shaking the walls of the penthouse before she fell into silent convulsions between them. Hecate eased the pressure on Seph's clit, allowing her to ride out her orgasm and make a mess of Hades' lap.

Though Seph eventually caught her breath, she did not catch a break.

She blinked, and then she was on the floor, Hecate spinning her around to face Hades, who was already sitting at the edge of the bed. He grabbed a fistful of her curls now and drew her closer. The look in his eyes made her thighs tremble.

He and Hecate entered her at the same time, Hades plunging his cock down her throat while Hecate buried her dildo in Seph's cunt, their strokes falling in sync as if they'd rehearsed it.

It wasn't long before Hades was on his feet, filling her throat to capacity so that it was impossible to breathe around him. He knew her limitations of course. He knew how long she could hold her breath, and she trusted him to keep that count.

He didn't fail her, not in the slightest, pulling out just as she was on the verge of lightheadedness. Although she suspected he was more eager to hear her gag with each stroke than he was to let her breathe, his shallow breaths shoved through gritted teeth each time she choked and swallowed around him in quick succession.

He was holding out, doing whatever he could to keep from cumming too soon. She wondered if he could wait out Hecate by sheer power of will, but she wasn't willing to find out. With shaking hands, she reached around him and dug her nails into his ass while her tongue massaged the underside of his shaft. She reached up and cupped his sac once more, squeezing and massaging it with determined fingers. Hades roared, bottoming out in her mouth and holding her forehead to his groin for as long as possible.

When he pulled out, she sucked down air with desperate haste then took him right back in, moaning at the sting of Hecate's hand across her ass.

"She's really good at this," Hecate breathed.

"That, she is," Hades growled, and although her eyes were rolling back in her head, Persephone could imagine the proud look on his face. It made her moan around him. "You've been missing this, huh, baby?"

She moaned out again in the affirmative, but it swiftly turned into a cry that nearly had her biting into Hades. The toy was back against her clit, and any control she had reclaimed was ripped away. She was certain she would be consumed by another orgasm at any moment. However, she wasn't the next one to cum.

Again, her attention had been torn from its prior focus, her mind now fixed on the vibrations ravaging her pussy. Even as Hades fucked her throat mercilessly, she was oblivious to the way he jerked and twitched out of rhythm.

"Fuck, Seph!"

His voice boomed around them as he bottomed out again, his first orgasm claiming him in an iron grip. He held her in place, but she continued to suck and lick him, dragging every possible sound out of his pretty mouth until he finally collapsed back on the bed.

Seph jolted forward, biting down on his thigh and earning a shout as she came too, throwing her hips back into Hecate's. Hecate grunted with her own exertion, gripping Seph's thighs and driving into her. Hecate's moans began to build, cutting through the air until they abruptly broke off, severed by the tremors ravaging her body. Her thrusts were sharp and erratic, and Seph could only imagine the look on her face as she joined them in ecstasy. The pleasure was so immense that Seph felt like she might burst into a billion stars what with the heat burning within and throughout. She could hardly take it anymore. And yet, she could not get enough.

When her body had again recovered some, Persephone slumped on top of Hades, who pulled her up onto his chest. Hecate stood on shaky legs, turning off the vibrator and setting it back on the bedside table. Persephone tried to turn and see what she was doing, but then Hades was rolling over, placing her on her back before pushing himself to his feet.

"Pick one."

He gestured to the bedside table, more specifically the dildo collection on the bedside table, staring at her. Persephone inhaled sharply, propping herself up on her elbows and looking over the options. She was already growing sore between her thighs, the delicious bruises of possession beginning to bloom. Still, she pointed at the thickest one on the end, a baby blue model that was just as long as Hades at least. Hecate picked it up, swapping it out with the current one before Hades drove her towards the bed. He obviously wasn't going to be passive any longer.

"You think you can go another round, baby?"

His voice was cool and coaxing, washing over Persephone like spring rain. She laid back and spread her thighs apart with a nod.

"Tell you what." He gripped his shaft. "You let Hecate cum first, and I'll give you one more gift."

She was nodding before he even finished the sentence, hooking an ankle around Hecate's hip and dragging her forth onto the bed. Hecate all but fell into her, sinking into her pussy and making her groan. Hades watched as Hecate leaned over Seph, pinning her hands to the bed and throwing her hips into her relentlessly. He let them get comfortable before climbing atop the mattress behind them, pressing a hand between Hecate's shoulder blades and bending her forward further.

He teased her folds with the tip of his cock, her hips stuttering in response. Persephone's hands wrapped around her, gripping her ass and spreading her open for him. Her lips and thighs were slick with her need, and he slid right into her pussy, her walls rippling around him. He needn't do a thing else, her hips swinging between them eagerly like a wrecking ball. She had been yearning for this level of control all along, and as she sped up, both her and Persephone cried out louder and longer.

Hades reached down, taking up Persephone's ankles and stretching out his arms, leaving her wide open for Hecate's stroke.

"Fuck!" Persephone sobbed, her hands swatting at Hecate's ass before they were clutching her shoulders. "Yes! Yes!"

Then Hades was moving, ramming into Hecate who in turned rammed into Persephone until they were once again that well-oiled machine, moving in unison while their sounds danced together in the air.

"Remember what I said," Hades managed. "You better not cum, babygirl."

"Fuck!" Persephone shouted again, her nails threatening to draw blood from Hecate's umber skin now. "Cum, Hecate. Please! Cum for him, for me!"

"I'm not - I'm not..."

But Hecate couldn't finish, not with Persephone's hands shooting down to tug up on her harness, effectively pressing the bulb harder into her clit. Her shout cracked across the space like lightning, her hips stumbling over their rhythm in a way that had Hades stalling out for a moment.

Still, she was trying to fight it, trying to make Persephone cum first and end the game. Persephone ducked her head and took one of Hecate's nipples in her mouth, tugging hard at it with her teeth. She may as well have pulled the plug because Hecate was immediately falling apart, clinging to Persephone as she writhed then withered between them.

Hades needed no help rolling them over so that Persephone was now on top of Hecate, both of them spilling a slew of curses in their wake. Persephone's morphed into a mess of moans as he kneeled down and lapped at her folds, dragging it upward towards her ass.

"Hades..."

She reached back, gripping a cheek and giving him more room, his tongue swirling around her hole thoroughly. She rocked on Hecate's strap, the other woman marking up her neck with hungry kisses and rough bites. Hades took his time tonguing her down, edging her again and again, making her whimper and weep with frustration.

"Hades! Please!"

To her surprise, he didn't take that as a challenge to hold out longer. Instead, he gave her one last good lick before pulling out and straightening up. She anxiously anticipated his entry, continually grinding her hips down into Hecate's, but she was still caught off guard when he drove into her ass. And just as grateful.

He took control of her hips, rotating them through each stroke of the two shafts inside of her. He and Hecate pressed up into one another, leaving Seph utterly helpless and completely consumed.

She collapsed against Hecate, fingers curling into the sheets beneath them, urging Hades on in between her cries. He didn't waste a moment, placing a foot on the bed and fucking her like she'd offended him. Again, her eyes were lost to the back of her skull, a banshee wail reverberating off the walls as Hecate's strokes somehow hit a whole new depth.

"Okay, babygirl," Hades snarled on one particularly long stroke that had her jumping. "Now you have permission to cum."

All was lost after that. It first became a race between Hades and Hecate, but it soon evolved into a coordinated effort, the two of them repeatedly hitting her most sensitive spots until she was wiggling her own hips in panicked desperation, her orgasm extending its ruthless hands towards her. It swept her up all at once, her back going rigid on Hades downstroke and her eyes fluttering shut on Hecate's upstroke. She couldn't even scream, her vocal chords frozen and her body pinned in place by unbridled pleasure. She came down in a fit of tremors, squeezing around both of them over and over and pulling Hades over the edge in the process. She shuddered and squeaked, hugging Hecate as he rode out his orgasm with a staggered stroke then a slow grind of his hips.

They wound up all on their sides once the world righted itself again, Persephone smashed in between them as they caught their breath.

"Was that a satisfactory gift?" Hades questioned, brushing Seph's curls from her face.

"Satisfactory doesn't even begin to cover how good that was," she sighed, doing the same for Hecate and pushing loose strands from her forehead. "How long have you been planning that?"

"Since before you left." Hecate shrugged, her eyes closed.

"I shouldn't even be surprised."

"You're right, you shouldn't."

"You spoil me."

"It was well earned," Hades assured her, wrapping his arm around her waist. "And just think. You'll get even more of that now."

"Please," Hecate snorted. "As if work has ever kept you two from burning holes in every piece of furniture you own."

Persephone laughed, nodding in admission. "That's true."

"Either way." Hecate opened her eyes now with a smile. "We're very proud of you, Seph."

"I can tell." Persephone smirked, gripping Hades' head as he kissed her neck. "And I very much appreciate it... Maybe I should go away more—"

"Absolutely not," Hades immediately snapped. "This is the only time it gets rewarded."

Persephone giggled, pulling both of them closer as her eyes slid closed. Even as she'd said it, she knew she never wanted to be that far away from them again and certainly not for that long, but this definitely made the trip worth it. Then again, Hades always made the hardest things worth it. She supposed that was why she fell for him in the first place.

"Okay," she huffed, wiggling her hips. "I'm ready for the next round."

Hades and Hecate both groaned although their hips moved too, and she knew she truly would need those two days.

ACKNOWLEDGMENTS

I want to thank each one of my Patreon subscribers, many of which who have stuck with me for years despite writer burnout, personal strife, imposter syndrome, and other general lags in activity. It is because of you that I am able to continue writing full-time and why I have yet to give up. Knowing that you are so invested in the worlds and characters I've created is what keeps me going, and I can never thank you enough!

# ABOUT THE AUTHOR

A profound lover of love, R.M. Virtues is an Afro-Native (Nahua), Two-Spirit bestselling author of romantasy & paranormal romance filled with mythology, fairy tales, and folklore. When not writing, R.M. can be found watching horror movies, playing rpg video games, or falling down a research rabbit hole.

You can currently find him online at rmvirtues.com or @rmvirtues on Twitter, Instagram, TikTok, and Patreon.

# Also by R.M. Virtues

GODS OF HUNGER SERIES

Drag Me Up (#1)

Keep Me Close (#2)

Let Me In (#3)

Love Me Now (#4)

SERIES OF SACRILEGIOUS EVENTS

Sing Me to Sleep

Divine Intervention (Black Rose Auction)

STANDALONES

What Are the Odds?

Claiming Mrs. Claus

www.ingramcontent.com/pod-product-compliance
Lightning Source LLC
LaVergne TN
LVHW010625100826
845148LV00014B/3111

* 9 7 8 1 7 3 6 7 4 5 4 9 6 *